THE
RING
ACADEMY

THE
TRIALS
OF
IMOGENE
SOL

OTHER BOOKS BY CL WALTERS

Cantos Series

Swimming Sideways
The Ugly Truth
The Bones of Who We Are
The Messy Truth About Love

Small Town, USA Series

The Stories Stars Tell
In the Echo of this Ghost Town
When the Echo Answers

Adult Romance

The Letters She Left Behind

THE
RING
ACADEMY

THE TRIALS OF IMOGENE SOL

CL WALTERS

MP PRESS

Honolulu, HI

The Ring Academy: The Trials of Imogene Sol
by CL Walters
©2023 CL Walters
w/ Mixed Plate Press
Honolulu, Hawaii
cover art: Violet Book Design
Internal Character Art: Danilo García

Library of Congress Control Number: 2023912639

Print: 979-8-9850325-6-7
eBook: 979-8-9850325-7-4

To our found families—those that we choose and those who choose us—the meaning of life becomes clearer because you're walking it with us.

Imogene Sol is for you.

BELLENIUM SYSTEM

Spiral Galaxy with five known independent systems and eleven habitable planets.

System Akros: Habitable: Drand & Carnos

System Rykin: Habitable: Lavi 1, 2 & 3

System Enoz: Habitable: Hommash I

System Ngall: Habitable: Serta & Ozmo

System Ares: Habitable: Slegmus IV, Inmara II, & Tolo.

THE RING ACADEMY

- Founded in 65G2 UFB (United Federation of Billenium System), the Academy is located on Serta in the Ngall System. With 2 centuries of tradition, it is one of the most prestigious Federation schools in the galaxy; only The Centurion in the capital city of Reblion ranks higher.

- It is a 7-year program. First year (Y1) acceptance is at 15/16 & there are two more entry points Y2, and Y3. Y4-7 are considered "upperclassmen." Year 7 (age 21/22) cadets are just below halos (trainers) & are offered the benefit of rank at the academy.

- Scholarships are offered for those who qualify.

- Each student is competing for the choice positions in the Federation——specifically within their "recruit class". From Year 1-7, students are ranked based on intellect, physical ability, & leadership potential. Students begin receiving offers for placement as early as Y5.

- An important Ring tradition is the Year 7 Trials. This is a rite of passage at the school before Federation promotion and serves to help those not in placements "highlight" their abilities.

- The Trials consist of the Trial by Chaos, the Trial of Acumen, the Trial of Tenacity, & the Trial by Examination.

1

FOCUS

Imogene raced across the room to grab the bo staff leaning against the wall, her opponent just steps behind her. The zip of his staff buzzed the air near her head as she ducked, rolled across the mat, and grabbed the weapon she needed from the holder. She turned and crouched with her back to the wall, wielding her staff to block her attacker. The clack of his weapon against hers vibrated up her arm through her elbow, jarring her teeth, but she ignored the discomfort—she was used to it—and shot forward.

"That's all you've got?" She smirked at her opponent.

Vempur growled, showing his sharp incisors. His stark, black hair curled against his umber-toned temple slick with sweat as he followed it up by stabbing the end of the staff toward her face. His eyes, usually green flecked with sparkles of gold, turned completely black as he swung.

She blocked and went for a jab.

Vempur parried, then swung the staff at her head, once more with a loud grunt and frustrated huff. "You're too quick," he snapped.

Imogene smiled at her best friend but subdued the laugh. She knew he wouldn't take it well in the middle of a fight. Not with everyone watching. Their silent, judgmental gazes were enough of a deterrent to keep Vempur's temper in check. Besides, she wouldn't have appreciated his humor at the moment either. There was too much on the line.

"You're stronger. Taller," she grunted out as she ducked once more. It wasn't to feed his ego. "Find my weakness."

"What weakness?" he snapped, frustrated more with

himself than her, it would seem. "You haven't lost yet today."

"Exactly. I'm tired."

Vempur growled, surging forward.

But she couldn't afford to lose and that was the difference.

She rocked back, arching as the staff narrowly missed her gut, then swung her stick out to catch Vempur's feet. He jumped and brought his bow down to the mat barely missing her back as she rolled out from under his strike.

"Stars!" Halo Mins—their instructor—yelled across the sparring room. "It shouldn't look like a dance. It should look like a fight!"

Several of the other Year Sevens in the room snickered, and she knew it was at their expense.

"Shit," Imogene swore, resetting as she hopped away. "He's going to knock me down."

"He won't. He can't." Vempur punched out, and Imogene blocked the weapon. They pushed against one another and locked, resting for a beat. "You've dominated everyone today."

"Not everyone." She pushed, using her momentum to twist and swing, the pole wide, catching Vempur's ankles. His giant frame slammed against the mat, and she went in for the kill, feigning a stab into his throat.

Vempur opened his hands against his bow staff in supplication and frowned. "Everyone knows you belong on the leaderboard, Imogene."

"You're partial."

"Sol! Neiklot! That wasn't good enough!" Mins yelled and stalked across the mat toward them. "If your trial was using the staff, you'd fail. But I'll give you that an audience would stand and clap for your riveting performance."

The rest of the students laughed.

"Neiklot, you're so much taller than Sol, she shouldn't be able to get inside with her reach. How the Carnos did she beat you?" It was safe to say, Mins was angry as he continued to rant, cataloging their weakness and failures, though Imogene couldn't think of a time when Mins wasn't doing that when it came to her. The sight of her seemed to set him off, as her name—Sol—set off so many when they met her. She probably should change her name, only she couldn't until she achieved legal status as a Federation employee.

Imogene widened her eyes at Vempur to communicate her incredulity at the teacher's comments, a look they'd perfected over the last six years at the Academy and extended her hand to help him. He smirked and got to his feet. They both turned to look at Mins.

At his full height, Vempur was at least a foot taller, her head only reaching his wide shoulders. He'd grown into his Astra-Felleen features. His big, wide eyes, green now because he was looking at her, were more often filled completely black, which occurred under heightened emotions in a Felleen. His brows hung heavily over those eyes, especially when he was irritated, which was most of the time. But whereas many Felleens had narrow faces and narrow features, Vempur's human qualities showed through. His face was broad through his cheeks and sculpted through his wide jaw. Where most Felleens had a narrow, flatter nose, Vempur's was decidedly human, a touch wider, crooked, and scarred from fighting. His sharp teeth were often hidden behind a nicely shaped mouth but were a touch terrifying when he growled. If Vempur weren't more like a brother, she supposed his features were pleasing.

And here she was, a tiny human by comparison.

They were an unlikely pair, she knew, but they'd found one another anyway.

The rest of the Year Sevens in their section watched with feral gazes, relishing their chastisement. It had been that way since her first year when they learned her name was Sol and all the jaded history attached to it. She supposed in their shoes, had she lost a loved one because of what someone's parents had done, she might feel the same. But most forgot she had lost her parents as well. As a Year One, their hatred had manifested into things like running into her in the hall, picking on her in sparring sessions, stealing things, and refusing to be her partner.

Vempur hadn't had it easy either, even if his name was clean. When they entered The Ring Academy at 15, they'd been alone. It had been clear many of their classmates had grown up together as legacies, arriving at school already familiar with one another. Given her name and Vempur being not only an Astra Felleen, but a scrawny, orphaned Astra at that, they'd both been the favorite targets of the browbeating. They'd found each other, fought together, and though they often lost, they'd been friends ever since, becoming the family the other needed. Now, in their seventh year, at 22, it seemed like a lifetime from those first days.

While their classmates' vitriol wasn't as targeted as it once had been, most gave her a wide berth. Some worked hard to undermine her with halos. The worst offered her their open hostility. She and her classmates might have aged, but that didn't take away their hurt and anger from what her parents had done.

"I expect better!" Halo Mins finished.

"Sir? How often do you think we'll be in a real-life situation having to use the staff?" Imogene asked. "It's peacetime."

The halo's eyes widened with incredulity. "Are you kidding me, Sol?"

She shrugged rather than say no.

Someone snickered across the room, drawing her gaze. She wasn't sure who. She wondered if it was someone on the leaderboard with her. There were 25 of them—four in this class—including herself and Vempur. She was on the cusp of slipping below the top five, with only a point between her and Dwellen Ridig in sixth place. Slipping below five and making way for Dwellen—one of those hostiles—felt like a death sentence.

Her eyes skimmed over Timaeus Kade—number three on the board—his dark gaze intense as he watched, his expression unreadable. Imogene pressed her teeth together and looked away, hating that she couldn't read him. She was also sure he was relishing her admonishment, as usual. They'd been competing since the first year, though truthfully, he'd never been openly hostile like Dwellen, just reserved and standoffish.

"I don't care if you use a slaggin' spoon, Sol! You will leave my class knowing how to use any weapon at your disposal whether you need it or not."

She straightened. "Yes, sir!" Besides the staff, they'd used twin daggers, knives, and a rope that day. With the Trials coming up, the review was necessary. Today, she'd gained the upper hand for each of them. Some by skill, but mostly by her tenacity. She couldn't afford to be knocked from her spot on the leaderboard. Her life in the Federation depended on it.

"Because of your impertinence–"—Mins turned away from her and Vempur— "Anyone think they can best Sol today? None of you have." He said it with disgust.

"Using the staff, Halo?" someone asked—she was sure it was Dwellen and knew he'd jump at the chance, though maybe not with that weapon.

Mins looked over his shoulder at her and smirked. "Your choice."

"I'll do it," a voice rang out, cutting off Dwellen, who she was sure had been about to volunteer.

Imogene wanted to close her eyes, recognizing the voice. Of course Kade volunteered. She pressed her teeth together, tightening her jaw but keeping her face even and hopefully as unreadable as his.

"Excellent, Kade!" Halo Mins clapped his hands together. "Choice?"

"Hand-to-hand. No weapon."

Imogene refrained from rolling her eyes.

"This will be our last fight for today. Let's see if you can go undefeated, shall we, Sol?"

Imogene watched Vempur cross the mat back to the rest of the Year Sevens, while Kade stepped onto it, drawing his dark hair away from his face with a band. She refused to allow herself to linger on the handsome aspect of his human face or the width of his muscular shoulders, or the sinew of his arms, or the grace with which his body moved. Who was she kidding? She was lying to herself that she didn't notice. She noticed. She was a living, breathing woman after all. Noticing was maddening.

"Gear, sir?" Kade asked.

"No. Let's make it interesting."

"But–" Kade's thick brow collapsed over his dark eyes. "That's–"

Mins raised a hand to silence Kade. "Sol can take it." The halo waited for her to admit she couldn't. A challenge, but Imogene refused to admit that. The halo knew that and would use it against her somehow, deduct her points, which would impact her rank. His grin widened when she didn't respond, then he said, "Ares rules apply. Take-downs only, a point for each. No face punches or low blows. Best of three wins."

Imogene rolled her neck and got into her stance. Kade mirrored her, and she couldn't help but admire him, objectively of course. She certainly couldn't admire him in any other capacity. He was taller than her. Not quite as tall as Vempur, but close enough, which made his reach dangerous. She was quick but no match for his size and strength. She glared at him, knowing he'd picked hand-to-hand because it would be the easiest way to beat her.

"Something wrong, Sol?" he asked. Was he just trying to rile her up?

She couldn't be sure, so she said, "Nope," with a polite, if reserved smile, even if the grin was a lie.

"Oh!" Mins interrupted.

Imogene glanced at the teacher, who was now standing across the room with the rest of the students.

"Whoever loses gets a deduction." He crossed his

short arms with a self-satisfied smirk on his face.

Slag. Slag! Imogene swore to herself and glanced at Vempur with a see-I-told-you-so look. She couldn't lose. Her heart sped up, and her brain began to spin with trepidation that against Kade, she might. She swallowed and made the mistake of looking at her nemesis. His facial expression shuddered, then was indecipherable once more.

Then Mins yelled, "Fight!"

Imogene used her speed to avoid Kade's lunge, hopping backward on the mat as her heart lurched up into her throat, threatening to choke her. She wasn't afraid of Kade. She was terrified of losing, losing her spot, losing any capital she had to get a strong placement. Her name wouldn't get her one. As her mind swirled, she turned away from Kade but miscalculated his movement, smacking against him.

He swept her legs out from under her, and they fell to the mat.

"One point, Kade!" Mins shouted with a bit too much glee.

Kade rolled away and stood to face Imogene once more. "Focus," he whispered, the sound razor sharp.

"Don't pretend like you care," she snapped, getting to her feet.

"Don't assume you know me," he snapped back, shaking out his arms.

"Fight," Mins yelled.

This time, Imogene focused on Kade's body, keeping her eyes glued to his tells. She liked to think that she knew her classmates. She'd had enough time over the years to study them—especially Kade—since she'd been competing with many of them since they were fifteen.

He had a few tells—though she figured he'd deny it if she ever told him—like the tension he carried in his shoulders and jaw he was always battling to relax. Or the infrequent way his eyes expressed the depth of his emotion when he thought no one was watching. Or the way he sometimes wiped his palms over his thighs when he was nervous.

He wasn't nervous now. He was focused like always, but she caught the subtle movement of his foot as he shifted his weight.

Kade lunged, and Imogene ducked, darted around him, and jumped, wrapping her legs around his hips and her arms around his neck. She secured the hold against his windpipe before he could get the break, then held on. Kade fell backward, slamming her against the mat to break her hold. Her breath knocked from her lungs, but she held on, unwilling to cede the point.

The ocean in her ears receded as she tried to catch her breath, and she could hear the yelling, a cacophonous eruption of sound, most of them yelling in favor of Kade. He gave it his all. Eventually, Kade tapped her arm.

Imogene released him, but Kade's hand remained on her forearm a second longer than necessary before flopping out to the sides.

"Point, Sol," Mins called.

Kade, his back against her front, didn't move immediately, his weight melting against her. Her breath caught for a different reason, aware of his body between her thighs, then mentally rebelled. Just before she pushed him off, he rolled—brushing against her thigh—stood, and held out a hand to help her up.

Imogene batted it away and stood on her own.

"Match point," Mins reminded them.

Kade leaned toward her. "That's more like it," he said with a cocky smirk, then resettled into his starting spot.

"Ready to lose?" she asked, taking her place across from him.

He laughed. "No chance."

"Fight!" Mins said.

Her classmates' yelling diminished until it was just the hollow noise of emptiness inside of her once more. The pressure of needing the win rose like the Cliffs of Mnor, but she forced herself to focus on Kade, and the tenacity she needed to best him instead. Her moves mirrored his, and she knew they were both looking for openings for their released punches and kicks. But as she maneuvered the mat, looking for a take-down opening, she couldn't find one. After several minutes, her own lungs grappling with themselves for air as her exhaustion began to take over, Imogene felt the worry creep back in.

She glanced at Kade and stalled for a split second.

His dark eyes—usually devoid of emotion—looked loaded with it, only she couldn't decipher what the look meant. She hadn't put any study into that.

He stepped back, dropping his guard, and giving her an opening for a take down, though she couldn't tell if it was on purpose, or if he was just as tired as her. Even as conflicted as she was that he might be intentionally allowing her an opening, she couldn't lose her spot. She took it.

Only as she did, her leg buckled. She grasped onto Kade and fell to the mat, pulling his full weight down on her, his hands on either side of her head. When he reared back, his emotive eyes held hers. The silence inside her stretched like deep night, with only the stars twinkling in the night sky, her body lighting up like those stars.

"Point, Kade!" Mins yelled.

Their classmates cheered.

Kade jumped up. "No. Sir. She took me down–"

"Your point, Kade. Judge's final decision."

Imogene sat up, her arms on her knees, and released a long breath, seeking to regain her center.

Kade turned back toward her and crouched. "Sol…"

"You won," she said, unfastening a hand wrap.

"And I'm three behind you now."

"I didn't want–"

Imogene got to her feet. She refused to show her struggle to him. "You won, Kade. I'll make up the points in the Trials."

"I tried to tell–"

"I don't need any favors," she said.

Vempur appeared at her side, his eyes narrowing on Kade. "You okay, Sol?"

"Yeah," she said, and without a glance at Kade— who still had that strange look she couldn't decipher on his face—walked out of the sparring room, knowing that deduction might have just cost her everything.

UNITED FEDERATION OF THE BELLENIUM SYSTEM

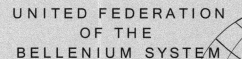

HUMAN

Bi-pedal species which walk upright, have a head with two eyes for sight, two rounded ears for hearing, a single nose to detect scent, & a mouth which serves to both communicate & take in sustenance.

Originally from the single-sun Elgnis System, their home planet— Earth— failed in 2967, & they were forced to their space colonies. From there, they explored, ventured, & colonized, bringing them to the Bellenium Galaxy.

They present as two genders at birth — male & female — though this identification is not paramount to an individual being's sexuality & identification, which is adaptable. Another variation of this adaptability is the human compatibility with many other humanoid species variations, resulting in Astra (mixed-species) variations.

This species is intelligent & communicative. Strengths include their ability to adapt, communicate, reason, plan, & persist, often taking over an environment to meet their needs with their adaptation, intelligence & ingenuity.

Weaknesses include their immune system, which is susceptible to virus & bacteria, & their difficulty fighting off such invasive species. They require oxygen & are unable to breathe in liquid or other gaseous environs without mechanisms.

2

TO GOOD FRIENDS

With another day behind her, Imogene walked into her room. The lights flickered on as she crossed the threshold, the door sliding shut behind her. After the lock engaged, she leaned against its slick surface and sighed, her chin tucked against her chest. She muttered a swear word, then another, and groaned before pushing away from the door, unbuttoning her uniform. It might have been one more day, but her days at the Academy were numbered. The final Trials were only a few turns away, and her ability to change her position on the leaderboard—now at six—was slim.

No room for mistakes.

Stripping out of her workout clothes, Imogene walked into her small bathing room. She drew the shirt from her body and slipped it into the laundry centrifuge for a quick clean so she could use it again the next day. After peeling her pants from her legs, she turned them right side out and considered skipping the check of her pockets, but breaking the centrifuge sounded unappealing. She'd done it once as a year four with a loose button, angering her entire floor because back then, they'd had to share. With the perks of having seniority, she didn't have to share anymore, but she went through the motions of checking anyway, shoving her hand into all the nooks and crannies of her pants for a stray item she might have stashed.

Her fingertips brushed up against something inside a pocket. Imogene paused a moment, her breath caught with confusion before diving into the pocket for the item, sure she hadn't stashed anything in her pants. Protocol. Breakfast. Courses. Spar. Workout. Dinner. When she pulled out a piece of parchment, thick, yellowed, and sinewy, her heart tightened then slammed up against the inside of her chest to restart a haphazard rhythm. Parchment—if that's what this was—wasn't used in the Federation. There wasn't a need for it with the tech available. Coms, readers, zips among other kinds of ways to communicate, the only kind of paper Imogene had ever felt was in an ancient book in Codex Hall where tomes were locked up. History stories placed paper as the turning point for the downfall of Earth.

Curious, Imogene unfolded the slip of paper, her tremulous breath attempting to find a rhythm. It was a tiny bit of parchment with a single word scrawled in black across its yellowed surface.

SURRECTION

What the hell was this?

Her heart racing, she took her shower, staring at the small scrap of paper lying on the counter through the glass, recalling every minute of her day, working through each action, and couldn't pinpoint any moment in which something like this—something that felt dangerous somehow—had made it into her pocket.

After drying off and dressing, Imogene shoved the message into her pocket once more and left her room to meet with her best friends. When she reached the door to Jenna's dorm room, she rapped on the black surface with her knuckles, then rechecked to make sure the bit of paper was secure in her pocket, glancing around as if she were guilty of something. Guilt was a strange companion. Unsure of what to make of it, she pushed it away. Since her best friends served as her advisory council, she'd figured bringing it to them would alleviate her bizarre reaction. She took a deep breath and put on her best normal-Imogene face.

The door slid open with a whoosh.

Jenna, human like Imogene, swiveled in her chair to face Imogene, grinning, her twin dimples deep in her cheeks and her hazel eyes twinkling. "Since when do you knock? Usually you're yelling at me." Her smile lit up her cherubic face. She had round, rosy, apple cheeks with wide eyes that appeared innocent (she totally wasn't). Add to that her golden hair and engaging smile, Jenna was adorable.

"I always knock. A yell is a knock. I just wasn't sure you'd be alone." Imogene wiggled her eyebrows suggestively and walked into the room, the door slipping closed behind her. She flopped on Jenna's bed. The room looked like most dorm rooms of an upper-classman who monitored a unit—just like Imogene's. A bed, shelves, wardrobe, and a desk whose perks included a small kitchenette and a small bathroom with the centrifuge independent of the hall. Jenna had her room decorated with colors that reminded Imogene of images she'd seen of the sea on Jenna's home planet, Lavi II. "Who knows what might be happening behind closed doors when you're seeing someone."

Jenna blushed and swiveled back to face her Com

glowing with the text. "Good thing you weren't here earlier, then." She tapped the screen adding the open document for one of her classes.

"Why? You did have a special guest?"

"Several of them." Jenna glanced over her shoulder with a grin.

Imogene threw one of the fluffy pillows at Jenna who ducked and laughed. "Oh?" She pushed a pillow behind her back and pulled another into her lap. "Does this harem have a group name?"

"The Fly team."

Imogene laughed. "I bet Vempur could make that happen if you asked nicely."

Jenna blushed again. "Stop!"

"You're blushing. Since when do you blush?"

"I'm kidding," Jenna said and turned her back to Imogene.

"Me too." Imogene studied Jenna a few more beats, watching as her friend made finishing touches to her essay and wondering if there was something she was missing. Jenna wasn't typically a blusher. She was audacious and funny, rarely embarrassed about anything. And though she'd shared that she was seeing someone—someone she hadn't introduced to the group yet because she "wanted to make sure it was a real thing first"—Jenna didn't often check herself. Of their friend group, Jenna was the impetuous one.

That's how they'd met, in fact. During a lunch at

some point early as Year Threes, Imogene and Vempur had been eating in the Globe, at their usual table alone. A norm. Jenna—who they'd never met—had plopped her food tray onto their table and sat with a vibrant and disarming smile. "This is okay, right?" she'd asked and proceeded to eat her lunch. Imogene remembered exchanging a wary look with Vempur, both of them positive they were being set up somehow, but lunch after lunch passed with Jenna returning to their table until that became the norm.

"Speaking of Vempur," Imogene started, "where is he?"

"How should I know?" Jenna asked, straightening her desk. A nervous tick. Imogene knew another of her habits was braiding her hair, undoing it, then braiding it over and over. "You talk to him more than I do."

Imogene observed Jenna adjust her Com, then readjust it as if deciding she didn't like it where it was and moving it to a new place on her desk.

"Everything okay? You only fidget when you're nervous."

Jenna turned in her chair and clasped her hands together. "Stop studying me. It's unnerving. And I'm not nervous. Everything is fine. Why wouldn't it be? How are you? Better than after spar?"

A change in topic. Curious, Imogene thought. "You already know how I feel. I think I expounded on my feelings ad nauseam at the Globe earlier."

Jenna nodded. "Understandable. And Timaeus–"

Imogene grunted at the sound of Kade's name and hated that imagining him made her body feel sort of weightless. "He knew what he was doing."

"What do you mean?"

"He picked hand-to-hand. Obviously, he would have the upper hand."

Jenna made a noise that hummed from her nose. "And how would you have felt if he'd picked something where he didn't?"

"Great!" Imogene said, her voice a bit too bright.

Jenna swiveled back to face her and narrowed her eyes. "Really? Because I can imagine that conversation. In fact, I think we've had it before. Damn him for thinking I'm weak," she said, dipping her chin to her chest and pitching her voice like Imogene's, "–and need an advantage." Jenna lifted her brows in challenge.

Imogene wanted to argue the fact but knew Jenna was right. "That does sound like something I've said."

Jenna smiled. "You know what I think is interesting."

"I don't know if I want to know."

"You sure do a lot of talking about Timaeus Kade."

Imogene opened her mouth to argue, but the words to disagree locked up. She knew they were a lie. "That's because he's my toughest competition. And he's always trying to prove to me he's better."

"Last I checked, Kade was in third, not first, which

doesn't make him your toughest competition. That would be Hemsen, Ravi, then Kade. Also, isn't that what you're always trying to do to him?"

Imogene harrumphed at Jenna, who chuckled.

"Are you sure he was trying to make a fool of you?" Jenna asked and shrugged into an aqua sweater.

"Why not? You know how it has always been between us–"

"True…" Jenna pulled a piece of lint from the fabric.

"And? Clearly you have more to say."

"You know I'm neutral when it comes to Kade. But have you ever considered that maybe he wasn't trying to hurt you. Vempur seemed to think–"

"Vempur? Vempur hates him. What are you talking about?"

Jenna blushed again.

Imogene narrowed her eyes. "When were you and Vempur talking about it?"

"In the Globe. You were there. We were all talking about it."

Imogene had been there, but maybe she'd missed it, too angry about having received the deduction and spending too much of her time looking for Kade to shoot imagined daggers at him from her eyes.

"Anyway, what I meant was that maybe things have changed, you know?"

"In what way?" Imogene asked, completely

confused by Jenna's trail of thought.

Jenna pulled her knees up to her chest, her eyes sliding to meet Imogene's, then back to the black fabric of her pants. "I don't know." She plucked at the fabric covering her leg. "Don't listen to me. I'm just rambling."

"I value what you have to say, Jens." Imogene thought about bringing up the paper but didn't, as if the words were being held back inside her.

Jenna smiled.

"You sure you're okay?" Imogene asked.

Jenna's grin broadened, and she shook her head, then nodded, leaving Imogene slightly confused.

"Great." Jenna's voice was a bit too bright now, and Imogene was sure something was happening that her friend wasn't sharing. But she respected Jenna enough to give her the space she needed until she was ready to share.

Which seemed to be right then, because Jenna jerked forward and put her feet back on the floor with a loud thud. "I got my placement," she blurted. "And I was afraid to tell you because I don't want you to feel bad especially after losing a spot today. And–"

"Jenna."

"There's so much riding on everything right now–"

"Jenna."

"–so I was worried…"

"Jenna!" Imogene raised her voice. "I'm happy for

you."

Jenna's eyes finally locked on Imogene's. "You are?"

"Of course I am. Are you kidding?" Which made Imogene wonder if she'd given her friends the wrong impression somehow. She leaned forward toward Jenna, who was still sitting in the chair. "You don't need to protect me. I want to hear what's going on in your life. Everything."

Jenna blushed again and fiddled with her hair. "I know. I just... I didn't want it to seem like I was throwing it in your face."

"You should throw it in my face, Jenna. You got your placement. That's amazing." Imogene grabbed hold of Jenna's hands. "I'm so happy for you. So damned proud!"

Jenna grinned.

"What is it?"

"Comms at the Federation–"

"In Reblion City?" Imogene's eyes widened. "Headquarters of the Federation?"

Jenna nodded and smiled. "I'll be working in the Chancellor's office."

"Holy stars!" Imogene whistled. "Wow, Jens. That's amazing. You deserve it."

Jenna nodded but didn't say anymore.

"Please don't tell me you're holding back because you're worried about me. I'm not made of glass. I want to celebrate with you."

Jenna launched from the chair into Imogene's arms. "I'm so excited," she squealed. "Maybe your placement will be there too, and we can live together!"

Imogene thought of the strange paper, but shoved the thought away for now, for Jenna. Her drama could wait. "Tell me everything."

Jenna chattered about the interview, and Imogene focused on her friend and her joy.

Eventually, a knock sounded at the door, interrupting Jenna's recitation of what she'd be doing at the Comms Commission. She stretched, reaching across her desk to the control panel and pressed the appropriate button. The door slid open revealing Vempur, who ducked slightly as he entered, and Tsua, operating his floating chair in behind Vempur.

"The party has arrived," Tsua said, raising several containers.

"He brought groff," Vempur said, his eyes meeting Imogene's, darting to Jenna's, then looking down at his feet. He leaned against the wall, slid down to the floor, then stretched his long legs out in front of him.

"Groff?" Jenna asked. "Can't. On duty."

"I can't drink that," Imogene echoed. "I have a test in advanced Inmara Coms tomorrow." She held up her hands to ward it off. "The last time I drank with you, I almost missed Intergalactic mathematics."

"Oh, come on," Tsua exclaimed. His skin pulsed

with various shades of yellow with a hint of orange, indicating his mischievousness. "Come on, Imogene. One won't hurt you."

Tsua was the last addition to their foursome. He hadn't been admitted to the Ring Academy until year three, the last possible admit year for acceptance. A mnemone from the remote planet Hammosh in the Enoz system, Imogene had never met anyone like him before. Truthfully, not many had. Because they required water, mnemones rarely left their planet. Their translucent skin that changed color with their moods and thoughts was initially peculiar, but Tsua's differences were his gifts. Brilliant, beautiful, and bullheaded, Tsua made the perfect addition to their friend group. Which was why Jenna had introduced him.

"Speak for yourself," Imogene groused at him.

They all groaned.

"It's only one point," Tsua said. "One! You'll make that up in no time. And you know someone is going to get a deduction before final Trials. You'll be back in the top five before you know it."

"Tsua, you have your placement," she pointed out good-naturedly. She wasn't jealous that Tsua, and now Jenna, had an offer for Federation placement; Tsua's placement was in ComTech as an engineer. She was happy for them. "You know how hard it is for me to maintain any ground. And you didn't see Mins's glee when he got to deduct the point."

"That's true. She isn't exaggerating. He was giddy," Vempur confirmed. He crossed his arms over his broad chest.

"Exaggerating?" Imogene asked.

"I might have suggested that," Tsua admitted. "Sorry, Imogene, but you can get one-track minded about stuff like that."

She tried not to feel hurt but did.

Tsua leaned forward, his life-support chair floating forward with his movement. "I understand why you do," he added. "We all have reasons, right?" He looked around the room at them all, each of them having lost someone they loved during the Dark War. He handed a groff container to Imogene, and she took it. "One in honor of your point then." He handed a container to Jenna, who said she'd save it for later, then to Vempur before holding one up himself.

"Okay. Fine. I'll drink one" —she pointed at Tsua with a stern look— "to regaining a point, but more importantly to congratulate Jenna."

"Right. Yes! Congratulations, Jenna," Tsua said.

"Congratulations, Jenna," Vempur added, his eyes fully black as he looked at her. He didn't hold it, however, looking back at the container of groff in his hands.

"Wait. You both knew?" Their looks confirmed she'd been the last to be told. "I guess I owe you all an apology."

"No," Jenna said, grabbing hold of Imogene's wrist. "You don't. You do have more to lose than the rest of us. So your worry is understandable."

Imogene held Jenna's eyes a moment, offering a silent thank you, and knowing she couldn't bring up the paper yet. Instead, she held up her container. "I'll add to the toast. To Vempur's and my forthcoming placements and to my best friends."

"Here! Here!" they all said in unison.

She glanced from Vempur, to Jenna, to Tsua, so grateful for them. Losing her standing on the leaderboard was a major deal for her, but with them at her side, they were right, it didn't feel like something she couldn't overcome. She sipped, happy to be with them because they made everything in the world feel just right.

UNITED FEDERATION
OF THE
BELLENIUM SYSTEM

U F B

Early colonization & exploration began in 2934 EY (Earth Year) when exploration gates were established between the Milky Way & distant space systems. Contact with the Billenium Galaxy occurred in 3256 EY.

A larger galaxy comprising 5 smaller systems, the Billenium Galaxy is home to System Akros, System Rykin, System Enoz, System Ngall & System Ares. There are eleven known habitable planets in the UFB (United Federation of the Billenium Galaxy)

Human colonization to the Billenium Galaxy began in earnest in 3291 EY but ended in 3407 EY when the Milky Way gate was damaged & decommissioned. It has never been repaired to reopen travel.

With the Billenium System interconnected by gates, the infiltration of Outer Rim System & the pressure put on fixed resources, a war broke out between the intersystem galaxy governmental system & pirates. This was called The Great War & occurred in 64E4 - 64E9 (3689 - 3694 EY). This resulted in the Treaty of 64E9 which developed the UFB. This governmental system elected a Planetary Council, an elected set of representatives for each habitable planet's provinces & a Judicial Tribunal.

UNITED FEDERATION
OF THE
BELLENIUM SYSTEM

U F B

 Every citizen of the Billenium Federation must serve 4 years in one of the following capacities, beginning at age 22 (through 26) as ratified by order 98.53C8a:

> WorkForce Blind: randomly assigned somewhere in the Billenium system to work hard labor positions (mining, food production, harvesting, dross refinement etc).

> Service Bind: Assigned in the ranks of Federation as cooks, cleaners, tradesmen, collectors, builders, etc.

> Recruit Low Level: Assigned in ranks of Federation as soldiers, fighters, province law enforcement, peacekeepers.

> Cadet Mid-Range: Assigned in ranks of Federation as low-ranked officers, planners, designers, barristers, accountants, trackers, traders, managers, trainers.

> Officer Highest: Highest level of assigned Federation Ranks: pilots, tech, leaders, ship captains, 4th Order, etc.

After 4 years of service, citizens may return to their home planet as a citizen, remain in Federation employ, apply for a new assignment in Federation, or apply as a citizen to another world within the Federation.

3

FINALLY

Sunslight was bright in the sparring room, making Imogene squint and casting the room in golden relief. She stood on the dark mat that stretched wall to wall in the studio. It was too quiet; the voices of her peers absent. She turned just in time to see Timaeus Kade lunge for her. She reacted instinctively, jumping back and twisting out of reach. "What the..."

"Good one," he laughed, and she couldn't help but

notice his handsome face, shining with sunslight.

Confused, she frowned and remained in her defensive stance, arms raised. "What?" She blinked, disoriented.

When she opened her eyes again, her back was on the mat as she looked up at Kade leaning over her.

"Wait? How did…"

Kade moved onto his elbows, one on each side of her, and settled deeper between her thighs. "I don't know why you're fighting it, Imogene," he said.

Her breath caught in her chest, lacking any retort to upset the balance of whatever was happening. Her body strained toward the pleasant ripples running across her skin, even though her mind was at war.

His hands brushed stray hair from her face. "Why do you hate me?" he asked quietly, his dark eyes skimming over her features.

Split in two, Imogene tried to reach for the half of her that was drifting up and away, the half that knew she should keep her fists between them. She opened her mouth to say just as much, but her heartbeat filled her chest, blocking anything else. That other half was overpowering the need to fight. She lifted her arms, wrapping them around Kade's broad shoulders, and pulled him closer. "I don't," she whispered back.

Kade dipped his head to kiss her, and the moment his lips touched hers…

Her eyes fluttered open to bright light shining

through the window into her room. The alarm blasting from her Com was an ax repeatedly splitting open her head. She squinted and grumbled, slapping her Com off. "Damn groff." Cataloguing the rest of her body beyond the awful headache and spinning gut, her heart spun in her chest, twisting up the insides with the remnants of a dream, a pleasant one.

Of Timaeus Kade.

She sat up, groaned, and reached for her water. "Damn groff." Two groffs in, she knew she'd crossed the threshold of too much. She wasn't sure how she'd gotten back to her room but knew Vempur must have helped, though she wasn't sure he'd been in much better shape.

Imogene grabbed her Com.

Fuck you, Tsua.

A series of sarcastic messages snapped back, one of which was a video message of Tsua laughing.

Her Com beeped with a new message.

Please proceed to the Sirkuhl's office prior to morning protocol.

Imogene jumped out of bed, then regretted it, her belly rolling. She pressed one hand to the wall and attempted to focus on the Com as she read it again. Then she dialed Vempur.

"Why are you calling me so early?" he asked, his voice rough and coarse with sleep. "My head. Stupid groff."

Imogene thought she heard another voice. "Are you with someone?"

From the other side of the Com, she heard Vempur move. "Why are you calling?"

Imogene noted he didn't answer the question and was pretty sure she'd nailed he was with someone. Not super jarring since year five when Vempur shot up and filled out his astra body. Then when he joined the Fly Team, it seemed like his status on campus changed with most (aside from Dwellen, of course). If he was with someone, she wouldn't have been shocked. What would be surprising, however, was him withholding it from her.

"You're supposed to be up anyway for protocol, and I got a message to go to the Sirkuhl's office this morning."

"What? Why?" He sounded awake now.

"I don't know. Maybe…"

"Your placement!" Vempur's voice was filled with excitement. "You're walking out the door, right?"

"No. I'm hung over, Vemp. Stupid groff."

"Snap out of it, Sol. Take a pill. Let's go! See you at breakfast. You can fill us in. Oh, and good luck!" He hung up.

Imogene's heart was a tangle of beats that weren't making sense in her chest, but she managed to button her uniform correctly, take the anti-hangover medicine, and gather her belongings for the day ahead. When she made it to the main office, she walked into the outer vestibule where Commanding Officer's secretary— Halo Castoring—sat. The human man looked up when she entered and smiled.

"He's expecting you," Castoring said, nodding at the door. He dropped his voice. "There are others inside."

Imogene nodded, too nervous to smile, and knocked.

The Sirkuhl's deep voice beckoned her inside, and when she entered, two others were waiting with the commanding officer, both dressed in the characteristic black uniforms of Fourth Order officers—the Billenium Federation Police Force.

Imogene stood at attention. "You requested my presence, sir?"

"Yes. Sol, please come in. Pull up that chair there–" He indicated a small chair, leaning against a wall.

Imogene retrieved it but didn't sit.

Sirkuhl Glyn was sitting behind his massive desk, his red Felleen skin a lovely contrast to the gray of his uniform. Though he and Vempur were both Felleen, Vempur's astra blood tempered his coloring to a dark umber, whereas Glyn's visage was the more common scarlet. His black hair was laced with white, cut short in the usual military style, and his brow was heavy and thick, prominently drooped over his bright golden eyes. The ridges that ran down the length of his nose were prominent, his serious frown comforting in the way of something familiar. The commanding officer offered her that stern look now, as if to remind her of her duty.

"These officers are here from the Fourth Order. Officer Mutez–" he waved a four-fingered hand at an astra officer, who nodded, "–and officer Tynos..." The second one, nodded his scaled head.

Imogene nodded in acknowledgement.

"Please sit, cadet," someone said.

Imogene sat in the chair.

"Allow us to cut right to the heart of why we're here," Officer Tynos said, offering a quick smile of camaraderie. "Your scores and performance are impressive, Sol. Fourth Order effort and caliber. We think you'd make a wonderful addition to our ranks."

"We were just discussing with Sirkuhl Glyn that you are being offered placement with our department in the Federation." Officer Mutez leaned back in his seat.

Both officers smiled. Smiled as if they saw her for her—not just as a name attached to notorious parents. Her efforts. Her hard work. Her persistence and drive. It was everything she'd ever wanted. Then why did she feel like there was a rock in her gut? Fourth Order was a respectable position—one that she wouldn't have even dreamed she could achieve, not with her infamous parents—only it wasn't her dream placement. Truthfully, however, she hadn't considered what her dream placement might be, only that she would earn one somehow. And now that it was here, the disappointment surprised her.

She smiled and glanced at Sirkuhl Glyn, wondering if he would notice her overwhelm, afraid perhaps she would let him down. Though there was no love lost between them for a variety of reasons, the commanding officer offered her a nod of respect as the meeting continued. Bewildered why she cared what Glyn thought, she hoped she expressed her gratitude—tried to remember offering it—but the meeting passed in a blur of information that she knew she wouldn't remember amid the rising tide of confusion inside her.

"Sol has morning protocol," Glyn stated after a few minutes discussing details. "If you'd please forward the proposal to her Com, so she can evaluate your offer. Sol, you are dismissed."

Once she was outside the office, she pressed a hand against the wall, needing something to ground her. Tears filled her eyes. She'd done it. A placement.

"Be happy," she whispered to herself, straightened, and rushed to breakfast.

"Fourth Order!" Tsua exclaimed after she'd filled them in, swishing a spoon through his soup. "Wow. That's…"

"Congratulations, Imogene." Vempur beamed at her. "Did they say where?" He took a bite of his buttery cakes and sweet syrup.

"It will be in the proposal. I can barely remember anything else," she said, shoving her utensil through the food on her plate.

"I mean, I don't want to say I told you so, but I told you so," Jenna joked.

"Told me what?"

"That you didn't have anything to worry about. That you'd get a great placement."

Imogene forced a smile.

"You don't seem… pleased." Vempur noticed, because of course he did. He often knew her better than she knew herself.

"I am." She sat up and smiled at her friends. "I am. I just…" She stopped speaking, trying to find a way to explain all the feelings rioting inside of her, and glanced across the room. Her eyes collided with Kade's, and she cleared her throat looking away, that dream hitting her right in the middle of her chest. *I don't know why you're fighting it… why do you hate me?* She forced herself to look back, to meet his gaze, only he wasn't looking at her anymore, and her heartbeat stuttered in her chest as her mind chastised her for being so indecisive. That wasn't who she was. She had a placement! "I'm fine."

She moved through the rest of the day decidedly thrilled by the job offer, ignoring the pull to glance at Kade in the classes they shared. She focused on getting through these last sessions before the Trials began, on maintaining her place, and hopefully reasserting herself higher on the leaderboard.

Nothing had changed. Nothing. She still had a job to

do. So by the time she arrived at afternoon workout to 300 sixth and seventh years assembled in the Grove—a grassy expanse of space—resembling the pulsing throb of an artery waiting for the starting sound, she took a deep breath, clearing her mind and focusing on her body for the run. She needed to maintain her position and performance even if she had an offer for placement. Keeping it was critical, and maybe Fourth Order wasn't her first choice, but it was respectable. They wanted her.

As she stretched, she focused on the stability of her feet, the strength of her muscles, the depth of air in her lungs. Focus became her mantra, knowing that the outcome of this run could impact the standings before the Trials began. If she could finish first, she might be able to gain her point back, regain her place in the fifth spot. Make the Fourth Order pleased they were sending her an offer. Maybe even get another.

By the time the starting sound boomed, Imogene was ready. The pack moved, and she accepted her place in it until the herd thinned. When it did, she opened her stride and asserted her position. The cross-country path they followed started in the Grove, curled down into the valley overlooking the Marken Plains, and cut back up through campus over the trail through the Cliffs of Mnor before spitting them back out onto campus until they circled back into the Grove.

The pack thinned further, and the leaders claimed their positions, those on the leaderboard predictably around her. Hemsen—number one—was in the lead. At number two, Ravi was just behind him. Imogene didn't see Kade anywhere ahead of her, which seemed strange, or Dwellen. The back of her neck prickled with concern she didn't want to acknowledge. She had moved into a tie for that third position, Sylar keeping pace with her.

Despite the concern she refused to admit to, she refrained from looking over her shoulder to see if Kade was behind her. *Focus,* her mantra repeated. *Focus. Focus.* She ran, her lungs and legs burning, but still she ran, slipping behind Sylar who moved into third position. The distance stretched between them as Imogene maintained her pace. She'd lost sight of Ravi and Hemsen as they pulled even further away from the pack. But she reminded herself she needed to focus on her own journey, her own place.

Footsteps sounded on the trail behind her.

She wanted to look. Wanted to know who it was but could guess it was a pack of them, Kade included. Dwellen, Lon, Bennisha, Fametly, or Sim were all in the top ten. It was one of them trying to overtake her place. She expected it. Imogene focused on her path, on the next bend that would take them past a deep ravine. The path was narrower there and being passed was potentially dangerous.

She sped up to create more distance, but whoever was behind her kept pace, either unable to overtake her, or content to remain in position for the time being.

The trail curled around the bend, an overhang of grassy dune on one side and the ravine now on the other. *Focus. Focus*, she internally chanted with her steps, working to keep her mind there instead of on the steps behind her. Suddenly, the footfalls behind her sped up, and she was slammed from behind. She hadn't seen that coming—she should have—and sprawled face first into the red dirt, sliding toward the edge and trying to catch herself to keep from toppling over.

The cadet behind her growled, "Slag you, Sol." Dwellen. "Fourth Order was my placement." He pushed her.

Someone yelled at the same time Imogene screamed, her body sliding the final inches of rocky ground over the edge.

As she fell, she grasped for something to hold, her hands and feet digging into the rough landscape until she found a tiny outcropping of rock on which to brace herself. Even though she was tempted, she didn't look down, focusing instead on the rock wall. The top wasn't overly far if she could find a way up.

Something was happening above her on the path. Sounds of a struggle, a fight. Pebbles rained over the edge, and she had to squeeze her eyes shut. When she looked back up, Dwellen was staring down at her, his eyes wide, his curling horns coated with loose weeds, and his blue face turning a darker shade. Someone had him by the neck.

Kade leaned over Dwellen's back, and snapped, "Fix it."

Dwellen reached up and tapped Kade's arm locked around his neck, gasping. "Didn't mean too," he managed.

Imogene didn't believe him. He'd pushed her.

Kade's hold released, then disappeared.

"Here," Dwellen said, reaching down. As he did, Imogene glanced at his outstretched hand, then to his face. He smirked.

"Fuck you, Dwellen," Imogene yelled. "You pushed me! How do I know you're not trying to kill me."

He jeered, his sharp teeth showing. "Suit yourself, Sol." He shook his head, raining the loose dirt and debris down on her, forcing her eyes shut again. "I offered—"

There was more yelling above her.

When she opened her eyes again, Timaeus Kade was looking down at her. She hadn't ever thought she'd think *I'm so glad to see him.* But damned if she wasn't.

"I've got you," he said, reaching down.

Her muscles locked with fear, afraid to move. She knew she'd have to maneuver her grip to reach up for Kade's offered hand, knew she'd have to trust him with her life. She also knew that if she didn't reach up and take his hand, the odds of getting off that rock face without falling were slim.

"I promise, Ima. I've got you," he said, his dark eyes

imploring her to trust him, bright with a new emotion she couldn't decipher but made her think of her own fear.

Her eyes began to water, his face blurring, and she looked back at the rock in front of her.

Slag. Not now.

"Imogene," Kade's voice coaxed. "Look at me."

She tilted her head as the water in her eyes dribbled down her cheeks.

"Imogene!" Vempur was on his belly next to Kade. Then Jenna's worried face next to theirs before she turned and yelled, "Back up!"

Now two hands reached for her. Kade and Vempur. A calm washed over her, and she took a deep breath to find her center. This was just like a trial, she decided. She could do this. With another deep breath, and using what leverage she could with her legs, she bent her knees and pushed off, knowing she couldn't miss. Kade's hand locked around her wrist. She wrapped her fingers around his arm and swung her other hand up to Vempur's. They pulled her up and over the edge, back onto the path now clumped with onlookers, her body draped over both of theirs.

"What the Carnos happened?" Vempur growled, the click loud in the back of his throat, his hand gripping hers hard.

Dwellen was what happened, but Imogene knew what would follow if she said that name to Vempur. The hate ran deep between them, Dwellen making Vempur's life Carnos for the first three years of the Academy, at least until Vempur's growth spurt made him more intimidating to everyone.

So she lied. It wasn't to protect Dwellen, but it was certainly to protect Vempur. "I slipped."

Vempur snorted, his skepticism written on his features.

Jenna helped Imogene to her feet. Her knees shook, but she refused to let the fear own her.

Vempur stood, his gaze darting to Kade with mistrust. "Did you do something?"

"What?" Kade asked. "No. I–"

Imogene stepped between them. "Thank you," she said, unable to meet Kade's eyes as he stood. He knew she'd lied, knew he'd been the one fighting with Dwellen. He knew what had happened.

But he didn't contradict her. "I'm glad I was there," he said.

"Get going," Jenna snapped at the Year Six onlookers who were now whispering, heads bent together.

The other cadets meandered away to resume the training session, leaving Imogene behind with Kade, Vempur, and Jenna. She knew it would only be a matter of time before rumors started. They would probably make up a story that she'd tried to jump. Imogene's throat closed, and those stupid tears threatened once more.

"I can walk back with you," Kade offered.

"No," Vempur snapped at the same time Imogene said the same thing, only her reason felt different than Vempur's tone suggested.

"I have to finish," she said and sniffed back the tears. "If I don't, next thing I know everyone is going to say I tried to off myself."

After brushing the red dirt off her uniform, and a failed attempt at trying to press closed a torn flap of fabric that had ripped open at her knee, she resumed the last of the run. Kade, Vempur, and Jenna remained with her, running as a clump back through campus. When they crossed the finish line, the last group to finish, Halo Rushesh was still waiting.

"Two of my leaders in last place?" The teacher's Zardish yellow-orange skin flushed brighter orange, dark around his cheeks with his anger. His blue-black eyes darted over Imogene's form, taking in her ripped uniform, her scraped skin, and his ire dissipated. "Are you hurt?" he asked.

Imogene shook her head and glanced at Kade, hopeful he would keep her secret. As much as she should tell what Dwellen had done, she knew it wouldn't do her any favors. It would enrage Vempur, and she wouldn't risk his placement. Besides, everyone would look at her like a snitch. That was the last thing she needed. She wasn't a snitch, but she was a fighter, and she fought her own battles. The only way to fight Dwellen was by overtaking him on the leaderboard once more.

"I slipped." She maintained the lie.

Kade didn't challenge her story, allowing it to stand, a secret between them and Dwellen.

She gritted her teeth, hating that she owed him now.

Halo Rushesh narrowed his gaze. "Two points deduction for both of you for your laziness," he said.

Imogene wanted to shout at him. She'd just fallen another place or two depending on the point standings. And Kade. He didn't deserve that, so she said, "Kade was just helping me, sir."

"You think it matters?" the halo asked. "You think among your enemies, they'll care if you're just trying to help someone out of the kindness of your heart?"

"No, halo," she said, then added, "but I think the Federation cares if their officers leave their cadets behind."

"It's okay, Ima," Kade said under his breath, so only she could hear.

But she didn't like it. She didn't like that he'd kept her secret. She didn't like that he'd lost points for her. Now she felt like she owed him, or worse, that she wanted to let her guard down to trust him. She wasn't sure which was worse.

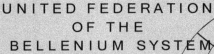

UNITED FEDERATION
OF THE
BELLENIUM SYSTEM

*A S T R A

The *Astra* is a marker for interspecies offspring.

Due to DNA compatibility of humans with many other species, many astra present as bipedal humanoids. However, this is not always an astras' presentation & cannot be assumed.

Strengths & weakness depend on each individual astra & the combination of DNA scripts.

* The demarkation of this astra rendering is the imagined offspring of a human and mnemone mating. Not all of this pairing will present in this way.

4

THE THREAT

"Twice in one day? That must be a new record, Sol," Sirkuhl Glyn said, his back to her as he stared out the window of his office. The beauty of the day was golden in the light of the twin suns: Makesh and Argos. The rings of Turnus glowed like brilliant silver disks twirling in the blue sky. That fact seemed strange considering she'd nearly died today.

As Imogene stood at attention next to Timaeus Kade, she was losing her mind that Kade wasn't going to contain the event to just them.

"Why am I still waiting for your answer?" Glyn demanded.

Her eyes snapped to focus on her commanding officer, who had turned away from the wide window overlooking the campus, tracking him as he returned to his desk to stand behind the oversized chair. Still dressed in his dark gray uniform decorated with silver shoulder knots, he set his wide hands on the top of the chair back and leveled his large black eyes on her. His wide mouth was thin and his red-tinted skin splotchy.

As one of the highest-ranking officers in the Federation, Sirkuhl Glyn had the power to make or break their life beyond school. While she knew he respected her rank, both as First-Class Cadet in her final year and her rank on the leaderboard, she couldn't be sure he liked her—or anyone for that matter. She was in his office far too often upsetting the establishment and his peace, just like last week when she'd argued with Halo Graplic regarding his assertions about colonization in the outer rim and received stable clean-up duty in response. It didn't matter what she did, she'd find herself facing his censure, more than anyone else, in fact. Singled out. She'd decided it was because she was a Sol, and her acceptance was conditional to additional monitoring.

"Sir. I wasn't aware you wanted an answer."

"I ask questions for my health?"

"I thought it was rhetorical."

He made a noise that snuffed through his ridged nose, his nostrils flaring, and sat. "It isn't."

She noticed Kade duck his perfectly proportional chin to his chest, but not before she caught him stifling that infuriating, gleaming grin.

She gritted her teeth and wished she could do him bodily injury. Maybe a swollen nose and blackened eyes would ruin his looks. But then, she'd seen him with a swollen face year one, after the veen incident when the boys had disrupted a nest of the stinging insects and got stung. She'd still thought he was cute, even then. She was hopeless.

"Can you repeat the question, sir?"

"I'll rephrase. Care to enlighten me about what happened during afternoon workout? Halo Rushesh reported you were injured in addition to placing last."

Imogene frowned. "I fell, sir."

It wasn't a lie, though it was an equivocation. She wasn't about to tell him the truth and hoped Kade would keep it to himself as well.

She noted Kade tense next to her, his elbow bumping against hers. She couldn't turn her head to look at him, but imagined his light, brown eyes widening, and his black brows arching over them with the knowledge she'd lied to their commanding officer. Imogene knew he'd look stupidly endearing.

She schooled her face, clearing it of any emotion. "Yes, sir. I tripped. Then Kade helped me. He shouldn't have had any points deducted. It was my fault." She glanced at Kade, whose eyebrows shifted over his eyes. "I checked in at the infirmary."

"Yes. I'm aware." Glyn narrowed his gigantic eyes, tittering in the back of his throat, and sat back in the chair.

His eyes darted to Kade. "And you, Kade?" he asked. "You came in last as well."

Though she wanted to look at Kade, sure he stood stone still and straight like the Baskin Monolith at the center of campus, Imogene didn't move. She knew his face would be as unreadable as ever, though he'd probably be pressing his jaw together, the muscles twitching as he did.

She chanced a look to see if she was right. He stared straight ahead, stoic and steady, at perfect attention. His beautiful face was carved artwork, with his broad forehead under black hair and his eyes, golden brown in the suns' light, framed by thick black brows, now impassive. His smooth brown skin stretched over full but sharp cheekbones that tapered to a masculine jaw shaved clean that hinted of new growth—and sure enough, twitching just as she'd thought, which had her suppressing a smile. His nose was strong and prominent from the bridge to tip, drawing her eyes to a generous mouth—a kissable mouth.

Imogene cut her gaze back to what was in front of her, annoyed at the direction of her thoughts. *No. No. No.* She wanted to shake her head. *Focus, Imogene.* The problem was that her preoccupation with Kade was happening more and more frequently. And now she was dreaming about him. She couldn't afford to think that way. Not this close to the end. Even if he had helped her. Her stomach tightened as she maintained her focus out the window behind Sirkuhl Glyn, afraid for Vempur.

Her gaze slid to Kade again.

"Yes, sir. I just wanted to make sure another cadet was okay. I couldn't leave a teammate behind." Kade's voice was deep and rich, and it irritated her that she noticed. And he was keeping her secret. Was she grateful? Yes. Did she trust it? No.

"And risk your placement," Glyn snapped, accompanied by a click in the back of his throat which was normal for his species when they became riled. The Felleen were notorious for their mood swings—which was why she worried for Vempur—but the involuntary vocalization made predicting his mood so much easier.

"I wasn't concerned about placement, sir."

Glyn took a deep breath, and with his elbows on the desktop, he leaned forward and placed his face onto his steepled hands, followed by the whoosh of his sigh. "Kade, do you have any information that is relevant to today's events?"

Kade's gaze collided with Imogene's, then slid away. "No, sir."

"You are dismissed then. Sol, you aren't."

Kade turned and exited the office.

Imogene remained still, her hands folded one over the other behind her back.

"Sol. Why do I feel as if you're not telling me the whole story? It seems to be a consistent pattern with you."

He was right, but she feigned ignorance. "Sir?"

He held up his hand, and Imogene had the sense that her commanding officer looked tired. Maybe she was driving him into an early grave. Was that more silver hair at his temples?

"You've dropped another place on the leaderboard. Do you think your placement with the Fourth Order will remain if you continue to drop? Imagine if that leads to a placement running a mine of Carnos." He stopped to let that sink in, and her initial concern for him dissipated like steam.

Carnos—the prison planet in the Akros system— was the worst possible placement in the Federation. Near the outer rim, it hosted extreme temperatures, raids by pirates, and housed every prisoner in the Federation. No one wanted that assignment.

"Do I have to remind you that's where everyone assumes you'll end up as the progeny of your parents? I would hate to have to explain to your benefactor how their advocacy was wasted supporting you here. Do you understand?" He laced his fingers together in front of his wide mouth, his elbows resting on the black desktop.

Imogene suppressed her anger. Throwing her dead parents at her like that, reminding her she relied on the goodwill of strangers was low, but she didn't contradict him. He was her commanding officer; his influence in the Federation was enough not to test him, and his recommendation in addition to the Trials performance was critical. She clenched her jaw and repeated her standard phrase, "Yes, sir."

"With the Trials impending, it could make or break your career. Is my meaning clear?"

"Sir?" Was that a threat?

"You have a lot more to lose now, don't you?" She heard the Felleen hiss in his words, a speech pattern of his species it seemed he'd worked to sever. For the moment, the sliding 's' sound slithered its way into his words.

Imogene bit her cheek to keep from lashing out. Instead, she focused on the pinch of her teeth against the interior of her mouth.

Sirkuhl Glyn frowned and opened his mouth as if he wanted to say something more, his sharp teeth suddenly more sinister, but he only said, "You're dismissed."

Imogene turned and left, pausing a moment after the door clicked shut. Closing her eyes, she took a deep breath, then looked up. Standing with his back against the wall across the hall, his hands shoved into his pockets and his booted feet crossed at the ankle, waited Timaeus Kade.

5

CRUMBLING WALLS

"You lied," he said. "And that isn't the first time."

Rather than admit or acknowledge it along with the fact he'd covered for her, Imogene deflected. "What are you doing?" she asked.

He noted her acerbic tone with a slight rise of his stellar brows.

She rolled her eyes as she turned and started down the hallway.

"Waiting. Obviously." His boots stamped against the shiny, black floors behind her.

"Why? To gloat? Because you kept my secret?"

"Actually, no. Why would you think that?"

Imogene stopped, and Kade walked into her back. She turned to face him.

He stepped away and swiped a hand over his chest as if to wipe away the feel of her.

She narrowed her eyes. "Are you kidding me? You've been angry about my presence on the board for the last five years, Kade."

"Not angry, Sol. Just driven." Kade offered her one of those winning smiles that charmed everyone. It made her grind her teeth together, especially because her mind went to the dream, to the perceived way she'd felt his weight on her.

"Why didn't you say something to the Sirkuhl?"

His dark brows bunched together. "You didn't seem to want him to know."

She crossed her arms as her mind spun. "What are you playing at?"

Kade moved closer, and she held her ground even if her first impulse was to step back. The instinct wasn't because she was intimidated, but instead because she saw weakness in her attraction to him. She couldn't afford any weakness, especially now. She had to work extra hard to earn her place back in the top five.

"Why did you lie?"

"Not that it's any of your business," she tossed back as she kept walking, "—for Vempur."

Kade fell into step next to her. "Dwellen shouldn't get away with it."

"Why are you following me?"

"I'm beside you."

She rolled her eyes, again, which annoyed her even further. She couldn't seem to stop when it came to Kade.

"The truth?" he asked.

"No. I want your lies."

He smiled and glanced down. "Can we go somewhere? To talk?"

The way he said it, as if to clarify his intentions, heated her skin and rushed from the back of her neck down her spine. Imogene chastised herself, keeping her game face steady. "Are you for real? The first trial is impending, and you think I want to fraternize with the enemy."

He grabbed her sleeve to stop her and spun her to face him. "I'm not your enemy, Imogene."

The heat of his touch raced across her skin like a wave.

"You could have fooled me, Kade." She struggled to look at his handsome face, shrugged out of his touch despite the latent desire to keep it, and remained gazing down the hall, jaw clenched. "And now you're trying to throw me off, so you have the upper hand." Then she looked at him with a challenge to deny it.

"So, I throw you off?" He tilted his head to the side and smirked.

She narrowed her eyes and willed herself not to blush. Her will wasn't strong enough. If it were a trial, she'd be losing. Heat now spread across her chest and rushed from her belly to that space between her thighs. "Everything about you throws me off, Kade." She said it with as much derision as she could muster. She couldn't let him win. She couldn't.

His jaw tensed, the muscles working under his skin. "Look Sol, this has nothing to do with the Trials. Not everyone worries only about winning." His honey eyes searched her face, and she noticed the streaks of copper in his irises.

"Not everyone has to." She had to look away, because she liked his eyes moving over her face and she was thinking about his hands.

"Dwellen tried to hurt you."

The cold truth of his statement pressed down on her shoulders. She took several steps back until she was able to lean against the wall. Unable to look at Kade, the bluster and insulation of the competition crumbled, then crushed her with the truth.

"Why?"

She narrowed her eyes. "When have I ever had to do anything for someone to try and hurt me? Better yet,

Kade, why do you care? Had I been knocked out of the Trials, that's one less recruit on the leaderboard to compete with."

"I like you on the leaderboard."

She looked up from her boots and locked eyes with him. His words and his voice—a lovely baritone that reverberated like music and made her heart skip—seemed genuine. But she didn't trust it. She didn't trust much of anyone, and not many had ever given her a reason to trust them. Trust got you in trouble. When you were fighting against the legacy your parents left you with—traitors to the Federation—that's what you had to do.

"Look, I want to help." The depth of his look mixed with the calm tone of his voice coaxed her to drop her guard. He matched her stance and leaned against the opposite wall of the hallway.

His interest didn't make any sense. Her walls went up, but her curiosity at the game he was playing sharpened her competitive edges, and she wondered if he had something to do with what was happening. The reality was that both of them were competitors. Perhaps he was a bit arrogant, but he had reason. He was smart, physical, and capable. With the impending Trials, however, why would he risk it? Why would anyone?

"This isn't about the Trials," he said, as if reading her mind. He watched her, measured her. It was unnerving.

"You've always been an open book, Sol."

"Kade–" she started. Did that mean he'd been watching her?

"Call me Timaeus," he interrupted.

"Kade," she repeated for spite, and he shook his head with a smile that communicated he knew what she was all about. She didn't like that. She didn't want anyone to know her that well, with the exception of Vempur. To be seen that clearly was to be weak and vulnerable. "Forgive me for trying to keep my place on the board. Most everything is stacked against me."

"Because of your parents?"

She didn't respond because it was obvious. Of course it was about them and her struggle to prove she was different.

His eyes wandered her face, his mouth slightly downturned with a frown she interpreted as sympathy. Her heart stopped pumping, then melted into her stomach. Sympathy from Timaeus Kade upended her resolve to keep him in the neat box of "competitor" and stripped her focus. She had to look away from his knowing gaze, so aware of him as a man instead of as her competition. Was she so predictable? Maybe that's what he wanted, since all the other ways to best her hadn't worked. But with the first physical trial looming, that could be a big problem. If it came down to it, Kade was stronger.

"Sol, I just didn't want to talk out in the open. That's

all. You have my word this isn't about the Trials."

Doubt nagged her mind about trusting him, but there was also the wisdom of keeping one's enemies closer working its way through her thoughts. He had kept her secret. "I've got stable clean up duty this afternoon after classes. You can meet me there."

Kade pushed away from the wall and nodded. Then without another word, he walked down the hall.

Imogene watched him go, admiring his form in his dark gray uniform, then shook her head and looked down at her own boots. Competing with him was all she knew, all she'd allowed. Though he was a formidable adversary, she couldn't remember a time he'd ever done something to prove he wasn't trustworthy.

There was too much at stake. She'd built walls with Kade, with everyone. Now, with Sirkuhl Glyn's threat of Carnos and her placement with Fourth Order in jeopardy, she realized she was going to need allies, and Legacy cadet Timaeus Kade—if his offer was legitimate—would make a powerful one.

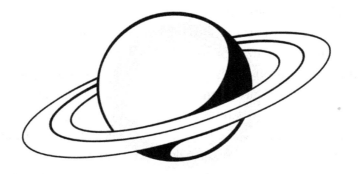

6

TENTATIVE ALLIES

"What can I do to help?"

Kade's voice startled her.

Imogene whirled with her shovel.

He ducked.

"Stars, Kade." The spade's head hit the ground with a jarring clank. "You know better than to sneak up on a soldier with a weapon."

"I didn't know you'd swing the shovel." He hesitated a moment, seeming to measure her, then walked into the stall, drawing off his uniform shirt.

His white undershirt displayed the muscle on his arms and through his shoulders, and Imogene looked away, concentrating on the bandon muck in the stall. She didn't want to notice him. "You just surprised me. And I'm on edge." She pushed the shovel through the soiled bedding, the sound of the shovel loud and intrusive as it scraped across the ground. It wasn't her first punishment in the sables.

"I think me surprising you might be a first," he said, frowning.

Imogene smiled and scooped, then carried it to the receptacle. The bandon snuffed from the opposite side of the stall, then walked toward her with heavy-footed steps. The large, stout creature, covered with a thick, light brown hide pushed against her hip with its wide nose. It made a low purr in the back of its throat, wanting her attention. "Stop," she said but pet the top of its head between its small, round ears.

Kade reached out and placed a hand on the animal.

She watched his hand lined with veins of sinew and strength move across the bandon's ridged back; the animal's skin twitched under his touch. Her cheeks heated thinking about Timaeus's touch. About her dream. "Here," she said, handing him the shovel. "You want to help? Make yourself useful."

He took it. "So?" He pushed the shovel through the stall. The muscles in his arms flexed.

Imogene crossed the stall to put some distance between them. "So what?"

"We're alone."

She'd bent to cut the twine on the new bale of bedding and froze. Alone. With Timaeus Kade. Her breath caught in her chest, and she choked out, "Excuse me?"

He laughed. "You should see your face."

That made her angry, and she snipped the twine with more force than necessary. "I'm glad I amuse you."

"You do more than amuse me, Sol." His voice wasn't filled with humor this time.

She glanced at him, but he wasn't looking at her. Instead, he was dumping muck into the container, and her body tightened with awareness of him. The way this shirt stretched over his wide shoulders and strained when he reached. The taper of his waist, the shirt tucked and belted. His thighs filling out his dark pants. She wondered what it would feel like to let go with Kade. Her mind wandered to touching him, those thighs pressed against hers, his hands on her hips.

When he turned, she was caught staring. She couldn't look away, and his eyes locked with hers. Even the clank of the shovel head hitting the hard ground didn't cut the energy arcing between them. He stared back, his gaze filled with more meaning than what she

71

could interpret.

"What? Infuriate you?" she asked and hated that her voice sounded weak.

"Among other things." He looked away first.

She'd won.

Had she though?

And what other things? She didn't ask, however, afraid of the answer. She knew she couldn't afford to wonder. She couldn't get knocked from the Trials, especially not with Sirkuhl Glyn's threat.

"So. What did you want to talk to me about?"

"Dwellen, of course." Kade followed her into the next bandon stall. She held out her hand for the shovel, but he waved her hand away and began mucking out the stall.

She gave the bandon some attention. "What do you want to know?"

"What happened?"

The bandon purred under her touch. She scratched behind the animal's ears and enjoyed the pressure of it leaning against her for more. It made her smile.

Kade stopped and rested an elbow on the shovel handle, his arm and hand relaxed, waiting. Watching her.

"I got an offer from the Fourth Order."

He stopped to look at her, frowning, but then seemed to remember how to be polite and said, "Congrats."

"Thanks, Kade."

"Timaeus."

"Why are you here?"

He frowned and resumed shoveling. "I've always thought it was a good idea to get to know your enemies."

"So you are here to mess me up for the Trials?"

"Why would I want to do that, Sol? You're one of the best competitors, and I want to kick your ass. Prove once and for all who's the better cadet. That means, however, you need to be in the Trials, and not out of commission because you're hurt. It's in my best interests to have you competing. Keeps me sharp, legitimizes my win. So on and so forth. I don't want there to be a question."

Imogene snorted. "I knew you weren't being charitable."

He stopped and turned to look at her again. "Why? Would you be?"

She considered the question. While she'd like to think she would, she knew the Academy wasn't built for it. It was a place to live and thrive or slip into obscurity within the ranks of the Federation as a squatter, and no one wanted to be the lowest ranked in the Federation. Everything about this place was built on performance. So he was right. She was as selfish as he was in wanting to do well for the legitimacy of their places on the board. Not a place for trust.

She sighed. "Fine. Dwellen pushed me, then said something like I'd stolen his placement." She stopped petting the bandon, who then pushed against her to remind her it was there. She stroked it again to keep her emotions in check. Emotions wouldn't let her think clearly, and she needed to be clear to figure it out.

"What a prick," Kade said, watching her hands.

She stopped, fisted her hand before turning away from the animal to spread the clean bedding. "Surprised? Seems to track." She cut another string of twine on a new bale and scooped up an armful of heavy, thick reeds.

"True."

She dropped the fodder to the ground. "And why were you behind me?"

He hesitated. "Just a slow start."

His explanation, or the way he hesitated, made her think there was something he'd left unsaid. "That doesn't track."

He made a face, his mouth mimicking the arch of his eyebrows. "Why? We all have off days."

She left the stall for the next one. "You don't." She heard him latch the bandon stall, then followed him with her eyes as he walked into the one she'd just entered. Once again, she held out her hand for the shovel. He waved her away.

"I do." He stooped, shoveled some muck and dumped it before stopping with his elbow resting on the shovel, taller than she was by a good six inches. She'd never noticed how tall he was before. Check that, she'd never noticed how tall he was in comparison to her before.

Hating that she was crushing on the man standing an arm's length away, she reached for the shovel. "Let me."

He released it, but not before their hands collided.

Her heart lurched in her chest at the same time she felt like she might scream. Turning away, she shoved the head of the shovel through the muck, needing to take her frustration out on something. How hard she'd worked! The sleepless nights studying. The endless hours of training. Using her wiles to get ahead of everyone else just so she could be seen. See Imogene Sol, the amazing Ring cadet, not the kid of the traitors. Now she was in seventh and Kade had dipped to fifth. Tears pierced her eyes, and the ground blurred.

"Sol?"

She didn't want his pity.

"Ima?"

She froze mid scoop, her back to him, then straightened as the tears started. She used her arm to wipe them off her cheeks.

"I just want to help." His voice was quiet and filled with sympathy.

She whirled on him. "Why? It doesn't make any sense. Not even that bit you said about the Trials. Me out is one less to beat." Her loud voice startled the bandon, who bumped against the stall wall. "We're competitors." She lowered her voice so as not to spook the animal further. "I'm your competition. I win the Trials—I get the better placement. You win the Trials—I get sent to Carnos."

He stepped closer, his face weighted with a frown. "What?"

She turned away and kept shoveling. "Yeah. That's pretty much what Glyn told me earlier. Said I'd lose the offer and he can't recommend me if I don't win. He seemed happy about it too."

"He said that?"

"Well... not in those exact words, but his meaning was clear."

Kade stilled her with a hand on her arm, a touch that burned under her skin and raced along her spine. He took the shovel from her and leaned it against the wall. With his hands on her arms, he turned her to face him. "Stop with the Trials. For just a moment." His eyes searched her face, warming her from the inside.

"Why do you care? I don't get it."

He swallowed, his Adam's apple bobbing as he did, and his eyes roamed over her face, stopping for a split second on her mouth. Letting go of her arms, he stepped back, clearing his throat before shoving his hands into his pockets.

She could see his mind at work but couldn't begin to know what he was thinking.

Then he looked up at her, his mask back in place.

"This institution is a legacy, and we're all a part of it. We can't have something like Dwellen's actions tainting it."

"Like me. The traitors' kid?"

His eyes narrowed, almost imperceptibly, but she saw it. She knew that Kade was as calculating as she was. He was intelligent, thoughtful, observant, and a closed book. These were all reasons she was probably attracted to him. But that eye thing was new. A crack.

He grabbed the shovel, turned away, and started scooping manure. "I've known you for almost seven years, Sol, and while you might be a stubborn bandon, you aren't stupid. You belong on the leaderboard without interference. You also wouldn't resort to such underhanded shit like what Dwellen did. You've got an issue, you confront it. Head on." He pushed the shovel through the muck.

There was something he'd left unsaid, but she couldn't fault him for it. There was a lot she wasn't saying either. But wow... if she didn't feel seen. Seen by Timaeus Kade. A new sensation wound its way through her insides, wrapping her internal organs with something dangerously pleasant.

I don't know why you're fighting it, Imogene...

When she was small, before her mother had died, before her father had been sent away, he'd told her to listen to the voices in her gut, the tiny flutters telling her to trust herself. She closed her eyes and listened, but what they told her didn't reconcile with what was in her brain.

Opening her eyes, she watched Kade before moving across the space for clean bedding. He helped her finish the rest of the stalls, working side-by-side. He didn't have to, but he did.

"Thank you for the help," she said when they were done.

"I told you I'm here to help." He shrugged into his shirt and buttoned it. "You might just have to trust me."

She didn't reply, instead replacing the tools they'd used before turning to face him. "Ready for the first trial?"

He tilted his head and studied her, but he didn't answer right away. Instead, she felt as though he were taking measure of all the things she wasn't saying. Then he nodded. "You know I'm ready, Sol." He smiled. "I'm always ready."

She narrowed her eyes, tilted her head, and said with a smirk, "There you are."

He studied her for an extra beat, just long enough to make her feel awkward. Then he backed up, his eyes on her. "You should probably try to win the first trial, Sol." With that, he turned and left.

After he was gone, she stood there staring at the cleaned-out stalls. The bandon had their necks arched over the half doors, snuffing and purring, wanting a treat. "What?" she asked them, but she knew they couldn't tell her. The only one that could tell her what she needed to hear was herself—and maybe the tiny voices in her gut that were telling her to trust Timaeus Kade, but she couldn't figure out why that would be so.

THE FIRST
TRIAL

This trial is an individual challenge that tests one's ability to respond under immense pressure. As an elimination trial, cadets are given an assignment that will test all areas of their abilities & future capabilities, drawing on intellect, strength, & adaptation. The trial is designed to narrow the year seven class by half. Those that fail to make the cut are eliminated. While some might have placements, failure to pass the trial will solidify placement as low-level recruits within the Federation.

TRIAL
BY
CHAOS

7

THE FIRST TRIAL

The slice of the door sliding open alerted Imogene that someone was in her room. Feigning sleep, she faced the wall in the darkness, her back to the doorway, and did her best to rely on her other senses. Quiet steps punctuated the silence—more than one set—the smell of soap—acrid but clean—the whisper of cloth—heavy and thick. She took as deep a breath as she could, ready to fight for her life.

"Up, cadet!" a loud voice shouted.

The lights in her room popped on at the same time.

Imogene jumped from her bed at attention to find two halos dressed in their yellow trial jackets in her room.

"Trial time!" one of them shouted.

The First Trial.

Physical.

Endurance.

Sirkuhl Glyn had led the Academy cadets through the opening ceremonies the night before between last meal and lights out. By introducing all the Year Sevens to the younger students, he'd hyped up the endgame showing what they were striving to achieve. He'd identified the top ten in the leaderboards which included her. In Seventh. Ugh. All their units had cheered their names from the auditorium seats.

"Move out!" the second halo shouted.

"I'm in my pajamas," Imogene said.

"Not my concern, cadet. Move."

Shit. This was how it was beginning: barefoot and in her pajamas? She supposed what better way to start a trial than to remind them of their weakness and vulnerability. As she left her room and looked around, however, she realized she wasn't the only one, which provided a small ray of relief.

The halos led her into the cold space of a study pod in Codex Hall. There was a stack of grays on the small table along with a bag marked with her family name.

"You have five snaps to dress and collect the goods that you'll need for the trial." Then they were gone.

She shoved her body in the gray fatigues and the boots, grabbed the bag and fitted it over her shoulders. The first trial would be one of endurance, though it wasn't exactly clear what that meant. She finished by twisting her dark hair into a tight bun and securing it with a band and pins. As soon as she pulled the cap over her bun to hold it in place, the door slid open again.

One of the third-year halos stood outside the door. "Let's get you to your transport."

Imogene followed him down the hall meeting with other Year Seven cadets all headed in the same direction. When they emerged from the building, they joined with more halos and cadets, a current moving in the same direction until all 150 other recruits from her Year Seven class were clumped together on the walkway toward the travel port. She scanned the faces for Jenna and Vempur, then looked for Kade, but she didn't see any of them. No one talked as they moved down the walkway cutting through campus.

Imogene had the thought that they all looked the same: gray fatigues. Bags. The only thing that set them apart was their names and their capabilities. This wasn't a friendly competition. Performance in the Trials could be the difference between success and failure in the Federation, and in some cases between life and death.

Her class had started with 180 recruits. They were down to 150, which reminded all of them that along the way they had lost students as either runners, eliminated by performance, dropout, or death. Imogene wasn't here to be friends and counted herself fortunate to have found some.

When they filtered into the travel port, her halo took her to the assigned transport. He turned and handed her a Com. "Here's your assignment. Good luck, cadet." Then he was gone, and she climbed the ramp into the small vehicle. Inside, there were three other cadets, four including her. She knew them all.

Loam, an AI Vispa from the planet Gosh, turned and looked at her as she entered, then looked away, focused on its stealth mode reader, plugged into its hearing port. Next to Loam was Hemsen, first in their class and a human recruited from the Outer Rim Space Station. His head leaned against the seat cushion with his wiry arms crossed over his narrow chest, making him look asleep. Imogene knew he wasn't. A loose cannon most of the time, he was frighteningly ruthless. Finally, Freidan sat across from Loam, a Binton with the most beautiful green skin and silky purple hair cut short to her chin; she was from the capital of the Federation. She glanced at Imogene, then looked away, rolling her feline-like, copper eyes.

Imogene sat down in the empty space next to Freidan across from Hemsen and belted herself into her seat.

The planetary transport rocked as it pulled out from its place at the dock. She looked at the handheld Com and glanced at each of her peers. They had their eyes closed, heads leaned back, or were looking at their own Coms. She selected human settings, pulled a set of ear pods stored in the housing of the Com now shaped appropriately for her species, set the Com to privacy mode, and pressed play.

"Welcome to the first trial, cadet," a disembodied voice said through the earphones in her ears. An image of The Ring Academy campus appeared on the screen and grew smaller as if it was following the path of the transport. "This will be a test of your physical endurance and your ability to navigate your way from a fixed point on Serta. Each cadet is located within a 40 kilom distance from the Academy. Your task is to use your wits and pack of supplies to help you return to the campus."

The Com showed the planet and homed in on the Marken Plains where the Academy was located. It stretched for hundreds of kiloms until it dropped off into either the Gadob Desert where the Canyons of Cintel were located, the Baskin Tribal territories, or the wide swath of River Rowe they called the Ribbon cutting though the plains.

"There are 150 cadets participating in the first trial," the voice continued. "Your performance matters, and the time with which you cross into the Grove at the arena will be tabulated with corresponding points. Each cadet has five days to complete the task, and only cadets who finish the trial within the allotted time will be allowed to move forward in the Trials. Your Com has been equipped with location identification, so should you need support, set your beacon for retrieval, but you will be eliminated. Good luck, cadet, and endure."

The recording ended. Imogene slipped the pods back into their port and the Com into the front pocket of her bag. She glanced around at those with her. No one seemed open to conversing, so she didn't engage.

"What is that noise?" Freidan asked a few seconds later, her gaze flitting about the transport.

Imogene listened. "That hissing sound?"

"Yes."

"It would appear the transport has been set up to dispense gas," Loam stated.

"For what?"

"To incapacitate us."

"Why?" Friedan's voice rose an octave, and Imogene could tell she wasn't as calm as she wanted to appear.

"Perhaps so we don't know where we're dropped," Hemsen offered without opening his eyes, hands folded over his midsection. "More challenging that way."

A few seconds later, each of them was yawning, even Loam. Imogene's eyes grew heavy, and though her instincts were to fight it, it was impossible. She succumbed to the dark.

When she sat up with a start, she wasn't on the transport any longer. It was midday, and the suns were high in the sky, blazing down. The reedy, rolling-hilled landscape of yellowish shoots offered no shade. Was it the same day?

She paused for a moment to check her body. She was hungry, but not overly so. She needed water, but her thirst wasn't dangerous. These clues made her think it was still the first day of the trial.

Half a day, Imogene thought. Four and a half left, she calculated. Forty kiloms. She needed to make good time. If her human body with optimal conditions could manage 20 kiloms a day, she'd be back at the Academy two days. First, however, she needed to identify where she was in relation to the school and give her body some fuel.

She stood and turned about.

The Marken Plains.

They stretched as far as the eye could see, the swath of grasslands stretching vast and wide with no landmark in sight, not even the curve of the Ribbon or the tips of Lopah mountains to help her. She needed to determine direction to calculate the location of the school. Without a landmark, she'd need a compass. Her pack was there. She opened the pack.

It was almost empty. Aside from three pouches of

water and a single food pouch, there wasn't anything in it—which seemed strange. Nothing for shelter or warmth. No compass. No light. Her breathing jumped with anxiety.

Think, Imogene. Think.

She checked the pocket for the Com which she knew would have a compass reading, but it was gone too. She looked around for it in case it slipped from the bag, but it wasn't there. But she was supposed to have the Com… to call for help should she need it. What the Carnos?

Deep breath.

She'd known the Trials weren't going to be easy. There was a reason they were designed to test the cadets. *You're in the top ten for a reason, Imogene. Think.*

She dropped into a crouch.

What did she know?

40 kiloms from the Academy. The directions indicated they would all be located within that distance from the school. Since she couldn't see any of her fellow peers, it stood to reason that all 150 of them had been dropped across the plain in equidistant intervals to one another, which would place them in a circle around the campus with the school at the center.

For the moment, direction was her most important decision. If she ventured into the Baskin Lands, she wouldn't make it back.

Turnus!

She whirled to find the ringed planet in the sky. Using it as a fixed position based on the time of year and the movement of the suns, she could determine her direction. So she waited, watching the suns as they moved across the warm sky. It was time she didn't want to spend but given the necessity to know which direction she needed to move, but it was the smartest choice. When she studied the movement of the reed shadows in relationship to the trek of the suns, determining which way was forward seemed easier.

She set out across the plains at a jog, which gave her little more to do than think.

Why only three packs of water for a five-day journey? Or a single serving of food, which she would need to conserve. Why no supplies for shelter or warmth? No one could make the trek in a single day, of that, she was sure. She reminded herself that the Trials were supposed to be challenging. Given her limitations, she wondered if she should power through the night. Without shelter, the suns' blistering heat took a toll until she'd stripped to the lightest layer. Waiting out the day and using the cool of night seemed like her best option, but without shelter and no shade in sight, she continued to walk.

When the suns hit Turnus's horizon, she stopped for a short rest. Her lips were chapped, so she allowed herself a drink of water and some of her food pack to replenish her energy. She wondered how Jenna was.

And Vempur? Tsua with his water trial? And Kade? With her eyes closed, she pictured him from the afternoon before, standing just inside the stable and telling her to win. She wanted to shake the image from her mind. It did strange things to her insides and ruined her preconceived notions about him.

A dark call in the night drew her back into her body from the sleep that had claimed her. Shit. She wasn't sure how long she'd slept. She looked for the marker she'd laid for her direction and got what little she had to keep going. Without a fire, without any number of things to keep her safe from predators, she was in trouble. She moved again, this time with more speed, considering the suns had gone down and the night was cool.

After some time running, she caught sight of a light in the distance. She slowed her pace and allowed herself some water, then moved toward the light. The closer she got, the realization that she was looking at another cadet's camp confused her. This cadet had a single shelter, illuminated by a temp light inside. That didn't make sense. She wanted to stop in and ask, but she didn't. Couldn't, really. This was a competition.

She knew it didn't matter and wouldn't change her current circumstances, but her instincts were screaming that something had happened to her pack. She kept going, running, making the most of the time she had in the cool air using her thoughts to propel her forward. A mistake, or was she the target of outside interference? But who would mess with her pack?

Sirkuhl Glyn had threatened her. Perhaps he had something to gain by her losing? But what? That seemed off somehow, her instincts rolling against that idea.

Anyone in the top ten?

Dwellen? Maybe. But did he have the opportunity? How? It didn't make sense.

A cadet on her transport? But at what cost to their own status as cadets if they were caught?

Kade? But she couldn't believe it. He'd told her repeatedly he wanted her competition on even footing, so messing with her pack? And how?

Who had access? A halo?

Mins? While his vitriol was blatant in class, the teacher hadn't ever gone out of his way to meddle beyond it. This level of this tampering was big, like lose your position at the Academy big. She couldn't see Mins taking that kind of risk.

By the time the suns began their journey beyond Turnus's horizon, she'd been over and around everyone who had a stake in her failure, but no real reason to do it. Every year in as long as she'd been at the Academy, there were whispers of hazing, but never during the Trials. Making it here was an honor in and of itself, something bigger than just the leaderboards. Bigger than individual accomplishment. She couldn't imagine why someone would take the risk.

She pictured the strange slip of parchment marked with that word. *Surrection.* Chills raced over her skin despite the heat. Something felt dangerous about it, as if it were a threat.

As the suns trekked around the sky once more, she rested, using her shirt to create a makeshift shelter in the reeds. She ate and checked her direction again, hoping that she was still moving toward the Academy. As she took another bite of her ration, she hoped what little she had left would take her right into the Grove.

It was harder to move as the suns cooled that evening. Her body and mind were exhausted and lacking calories to sustain the output of pushing herself across the plains. She walked and fought the exhaustion by counting and spelling words with each of her steps. She imagined her friends all moving in the same direction, converging on the campus, and pictured walking into the Grove at the same time.

She couldn't remember what day it was. Day two? Day three?

She stopped for water and took a long drink. One packet remaining.

She trudged ahead, her feet heavy.

Another light in the distance.

Another cadet with a single shelter. A temp light.

Imogene kept going, wishing she could talk to Tsua to help her reason it out. Her brain wasn't stringing together coherent thoughts anymore, just random points mixed up with errant images of the past, and faces, and feelings.

The next day, as the suns climbed to the hottest point in the day, she let herself stop, fashioning a makeshift shelter in the reeds. She couldn't be much further, she decided, checked her direction, and rested.

The crunch of footsteps woke her. It was dark. She'd overslept. Her heart pounded in her chest. Another cadet passing by without knowing she was there? Something else? After gathering her things, she started forward, trying to remember what day it was. She would have to make it back to the Academy soon. While she could survive some time without food and water, coupled with the physical exertion, she didn't think she'd last long. She used her directional marker and set out.

Lifting her feet for each step was difficult. The exhaustion from before felt like nothing in comparison to now. She'd been without food for the last twelve hours, having eaten the last of her one ration. She was down to the last bit of her final water packet, but she was buoyed by the fact she was passing more and more of her classmates bedded down into their single shelters, which gave her an added boost of confidence that she was walking in the right direction.

Before the night broke for morning, Imogene was sure the shadows had thickened on the horizon. She used the inky darkness as a homing beacon, keeping upright despite everything in her that said it was okay to stop. She couldn't, afraid she might not get back up again. Just one more step, she told herself. One more. Just one more. So she proceeded, coaxing herself to take just one more step until suddenly the wall of the perimeter of The Ring Academy rose before her. She moved as quickly as she could, which was horrifically slow, but moving, nonetheless. Just one more step. One more. The voice in her head was Kade's, though she wasn't sure why.

The suns ruptured the horizon of the dark behind her, stretching her shadow like a long, thin wraith guiding her toward the end. There were halos there, and younger students, all waiting.

When she finally stumbled across the finish to mark her time, she collapsed, the dark claiming her despite the rising suns.

FELLEEN

The Felleen is a bipedal warrior species from Ozmo in the Ngall System. They have a head, two large, wide-set eyes with colored pupils that turn black when emotional, & a nose used for scent with ridges from bridge to tip, two pointy ears for hearing. The mouth is used for sustenance, communication, & killing given their sharp teeth. Felleen warriors also use their hands (they have two arms & two hands) to communicate. With tall, lean bodies, their musculature is built for short-twitch speed. A strong & noticeable characteristic is their bright red skin though variations occur including a recent variation of striping. They typically have black hair, long & braided to indicate feats in battle.

They present as two genders at birth— male & female— though this identification is not paramount to an individual being's sexuality & identification, which is adaptable as necessary to survival. Felleen males & females are able to adapt their sex organs as necessary to maintain the species. The Felleen is an adaptable species, able to procreate with other humanoid species (such as humans, creating an Astra Fellen which might take on characteristics of either parent).

This species is intelligent & communicative. Strengths include their ability to adapt, communicate, reason, plan, & fight. The Felleen cannot float due to their dense bodies & must rely on mechanisms in the water. They are also susceptible to death at an early age due to their courageous but often daredevil natures. Felleen are not known to have traveled beyond the Billenium System.

8

AFTERMATH

The searing pain of her head was the first sensation Imogene noticed as she became conscious. The second was the presence of a shadow reaching toward her on the right. She blinked, correcting her vision, tense with the discomfort claiming her muscles when her body moved. She blinked again, trying to clear the haze. The vaulted ceilings with exposed beams crisscrossed overhead and long, narrow windows glowed with late suns' light as they set. She was lying in the medical wing.

With a start, she tried to sit up.

"At ease, cadet."

She turned her head toward the voice, and her vision sharpened. The commander sat next to her, slightly rumpled, as if he'd been sitting there a while. His legs were crossed, his arms folded over his chest, and his dark eyes studied her.

She eased back down against the pillows and pulled the covering up to her neck, worried as to why her commanding officer was at her bedside. "Sir?" It hurt to speak, the words clawing at her dry, swollen throat.

"Why is it, Sol, that you are always getting into trouble that requires my attention?"

"Sir?" she repeated.

The Sirkuhl sighed, and the chair he was sitting in creaked under him as he uncrossed his legs. He leaned forward, picked up a container from her bedside, and held what looked to be a cup of ice out to her. "You were severely dehydrated, suffering from suns' heat, and were malnourished when you crossed the finish line before collapsing. Did something happen out there that I need to know about?"

She accepted the cup. "It was a trial of endurance."

"Yes, but we aren't in a habit of sending our cadets out to their death, Sol, regardless of what you might believe. The Trial should have been difficult, but it shouldn't have come close to claiming your life." His voice was subdued, even concerned, which she found disconcerting; he was usually frustrated with her. He held up her pack. "It's empty."

"It wasn't like I did that to myself."

"I'm aware."

She looked closer at the cup for no other reason than to do something else with her eyes as she worked what had happened through her mind. It wasn't completely clear, but she remembered the thirst and her drive to finish. She recalled the confusion when she passed other cadets with supplies. Now, she felt the aftermath of fear, the realization of what could have happened, and shuddered. Her eyes met Sirkuhl Glyn's again. "There weren't any supplies in my pack, sir. I had three water packets, and a single food ration."

His eyes shifted, glancing around the room as if to find the answer there and make sense of it. "Truly?" He sounded surprised. "Each pack was provided with a single-shelter, temp light, a compass, and enough food rations and water to survive five days. You're saying none of that was in your pack?" He flattened his hands on his thighs and leaned back in his chair.

Imogene shook her head.

"And you didn't have your Com," he said as a matter of fact rather than a question.

She shook her head.

"We found it on the floor of your transport, fallen under the seat." The Sirkuhl stood and turned away, facing the windows across the room. A rush of air came from him, and he joined his hands behind his back as he walked toward the fading light in the windows. "I'm sincerely concerned." When he stopped, his head dropped forward. After a few beats of silence, he turned back toward her. "Considering the challenge you alone faced, your performance was exemplary, Sol."

"How long?"

"Sixty hours."

"Good enough? To keep my placement and avoid Carnos?"

His lips thinned out, his eyes narrowed, and his brows drew together in confusion. Glyn's head tilted to the side as if he'd asked a question, but he didn't voice one. Instead, his throat clicked. The look didn't make sense to Imogene. She was still thinking of the escalated threat and attempting to align her prior experiences with her commanding officer with the one standing before her now.

"There are three more Trials, Sol. You need to rest."

He moved to the end of her bed, and she followed him with her eyes. "I will be looking into what happened with your pack and determine if there were others with missing supplies. I have security looking at the video feeds now."

"Thank you, sir."

He nodded, followed by another click of his throat, then hesitated a moment, as if he wanted to say something else. But he seemed to decide not to, leaving the infirmary instead.

Imogene wasn't sure what to make of the concerned Sirkuhl Glyn. Angry and exasperated Glyn she could understand, but worried one didn't match her perceptions of him. She was adding him to the list of new perceptions that didn't align with all the ways she'd defined herself in relation to the world she thought she knew. It was confusing.

She turned to her side and curled into a ball under the cover, staring at the partition between her bed and the empty one next to her. Though her memories were still hazy, she tried to remember everything she could about what had happened. Exhausted by the unending loops of unanswerable questions, her eyes grew heavy.

When she opened them again, the suns had set behind Turnus, and the light glowed in the small sconce next to her bed. Jenna, Vempur, and Tsua were seated around her bed, talking quietly. Kade was there too, slightly apart from her other friends but listening to their conversation.

"I must have almost died," she joked, drawing them away from whatever they were discussing.

"Not funny." Jenna, on one side of Imogene, leaned forward and lined her face up with Imogene's. She grasped one of Imogene's hands. "What the Carnos happened, Sol?"

Imogene shook her head. "If only I knew."

"Tell us what you remember," Tsua ordered, his

blood swirling orange under his skin.

She sat up, adjusted herself in the bed, and relayed what she could remember of her experience from the moment she'd woken on the Plains through waking up with Sirkuhl Glyn at her bedside.

"Your pack was empty?" Vempur asked, his voice low and seething. He was next to her, opposite Jenna, his dark eyes studying hers, before jumping up to look at the rest of them. "We all had stuff in ours. Right?"

Everyone nodded. They listed the contents of their packs, all matching, confirming the suspicion that someone must have tampered with her pack.

"Except for the few rations of food and water. Nothing."

"And your Com?" Tsua asked.

"Woke up without it. Sounds like it fell from my bag when I was moved. It was found on the transport."

Kade, near the foot of her bed, stood and ran a hand through his dark hair, but he didn't say anything. He was frowning, which was a different look for him, one that Imogene couldn't recall. Determined, yes. Competitive, yes. While he looked as handsome as always, there was something about the concerned set of his jaw, the downturn of his eyes and mouth that told her he wasn't as calm as the rest of him tried to communicate. He folded his arms over his chest, and she noticed the way his biceps swelled, his shirt stretching around the muscle.

"Did you win?" she asked him, trying to keep her mind on what was important, which wasn't his muscles.

He shook his head. "Dwellen came in first."

Imogene groaned. "Dwellen?"

Vempur growled.

"Kade was third," Jenna said and grinned.

Kade looked down at the floor. "Hemsen was second. We all had supplies." His tone was angry.

"You were fucking fifth, Imogene," Tsua said. "Without supplies. That's—"

"Slagging impressive in as much as it's scary." Vempur laid a hand over hers.

"You?" Imogene asked.

"Twelfth."

"Jenna?"

"Twentieth."

"Tsua?"

"My time will be measured against the rest," he said. "Hasn't been announced."

Relief moved through her like a cooling breeze. Fifth wasn't the best, but it was good enough to hang in the top ten. "Well considering I had nothing in my bag…" she said, trying to make light of it again, but it fell flat.

"Don't joke." Vempur shook his head and squeezed her hand. "Don't. You could have died."

"I have to go." Kade couldn't meet her gaze, looking everywhere but at her. "I'll come back later. There's something I have to do." He didn't wait for any of them to say anything, just turned and left the infirmary.

They watched him go.

"Are we sure we trust him?" Vempur asked after he was gone.

"He was there at the finish line when Imogene came across, and he helped her when she fell," Jenna said. "He described it, the way you collapsed."

"The Trials are dangerous," Imogene said.

Jenna shook her head. "No. He was shaken up. I think he's been here most of the day. He was here when we got here."

"Are you saying that's why we can trust him?" Tsua asked. "Maybe he's just got a guilty conscience."

Jenna kept her eyes on Imogene's. "Maybe. But he didn't act guilty."

The statement hung there, and Imogene wondered what it meant. If it wasn't guilt, what was it? Concern?

"I can't believe someone messed with your pack," Vempur murmured. "If I get my hands on them, I will fucking end them."

Tsua's skin flashed from orange to black.

Imogene reached out and put a hand on Vempur's arm—she couldn't reach Tsua, who was near her feet—and drew comfort from her oldest friend's strength. "Not a viable option. I can't have you in Carnos."

A series of clicks sounded in the back of his throat, but whether it was from frustration or acceptance, she couldn't be sure.

Tsua's blood was swirling in his brain, changing his color, and communicating he was processing the information he'd received. "We need to discover if this was a mistake or intentional. If it was intentional, was it to harm Imogene's placement, or to harm her?"

Imogene thought of Dwellen. Of his anger at her placement. "Why does that matter?"

"Motive."

"The problem is we don't know the answer to that question," Vempur said.

"Let's assume it was intentional." Tsua looked between them.

"Because?" Jenna asked.

"Because I'm me," Imogene quipped. "Look, everyone has a motive. Even you."

They all gaped at her, then spoke simultaneously.

"Are you fucking kidding, Sol?" Vempur snapped.

"I would never, Imogene!" Jenna exclaimed.

"That's ridiculous." Tsua's skin swirled with black.

She held up a hand. "I just mean that it doesn't narrow the field," she explained. "What my parents did affected everyone."

Tsua blustered, his words catching before he could say them. "Let's stick to the facts. There haven't been any other reports of other cadets missing things in their packs."

"Or one item missing versus all of them," Jenna

added.

"Exactly."

"The fact that there was still water and a ration inside suggests that whoever it was wasn't trying to kill you outright. Maybe a fit of conscience? Or hoping you'd use your Com to eliminate yourself."

"Or hope for a slow, painful death." Imogene adjusted herself against her pillows, Jenna and Vempur jumping up to help.

Tsua's gaze was unfocused as his skin swirled with colors as quick and varied as his thoughts. "If someone messed with your pack, could they have messed with the Com?"

"The Sirkuhl said he's looking into it."

"Do you trust that he will?" Vempur asked and returned to his seat.

It was a fair question, considering he'd threatened her just days ago. "I don't know." The reality was that she didn't know anything anymore. A few days ago, she'd thought she did, but everything she thought she knew was crumbling. Things she'd been sure about metamorphosing into new things to process like Kade and the Sirkuhl.

"The next trial is in a few turns," Tsua said. "It's a test of logic and reasoning, which I don't think will exert you, physically." He paused. "Think you will be ready to face that?"

She nodded.

"I'm going to go see if I can hack into the video feeds," he announced, moving his chair. "I'll study the leaderboard and cross reference movements, see if I can find anything."

"Maybe look into who was in my transport." She shared the other cadets names. "And my Codex room."

"I'll come with you," Jenna said, stopping Tsua before he could glide from the room. She looked at Imogene before she left. "I'm relieved you're okay, Imogene. Let me know if you need help when they let you out of here."

Imogene smiled at Jenna and nodded. She turned to look at Vempur, who watched Tsua and Jenna leave, then turned his dark eyes back to her. "Please don't give me a lecture. It wasn't like I planned this," she said, used to his concern for her safety.

He looked down at his hands and shook his head. "I just... seeing you like that. There was nothing—" He tapped his heart, stopped speaking, and swallowed. "If anything happened to you, I don't know what I'd do."

"Vempur—"

"For real, Imogene. You're my family."

She refused to allow the tears smarting in her eyes to gain traction, but she nodded, and her eyes filled anyway. "Yes." She knew exactly what he meant. Vempur was her best friend, the brother she'd never had, and had been since year one. He was her family. She held her hand out, and he took it in his large one.

"I'll try not to scare you again, but we better figure out who's responsible." She thought about Dwellen, but didn't dare name him; besides, he didn't quite fit.

He nodded.

"And no killing. I don't want either of us in Carnos."

Vempur offered her a smile that tugged at the edges of his lips but didn't reach his eyes. "No promises." He sat with her a while longer, their hands linked as if it might chase away the truth of what had happened.

Kade returned that evening just before the medic cleared her to leave. He was alone but without the usual bluster and arrogance that often preceded him.

"So did you mess with my pack, Kade? So worried about keeping your rank?" Imogene teased, smiling to let him know she was joking as he sat.

"That isn't funny, Ima."

"I know. But if I can't poke fun about it, the reality feels a little too scary."

He leaned forward, elbows to knees, and ran a hand over his head, messing up his hair. "Fuck, Ima. When I saw you go down–"

"What?"

He looked up at her, his eyes heavy with emotions she couldn't identify, but he didn't offer any more words to provide clarity. Instead, he looked back at his hands. "This has to stop."

"I'm not sure what to do next."

His brown eyes met hers again. "Keep going. Whoever is behind it is trying to neutralize you."

"To what end?" she asked, her voice raised so that it bounced around the room. "Seriously. Aside from what I've made for myself here, I'm not a threat to anyone. What does somebody gain going after me? It doesn't make any sense. Why not sabotage anyone else in the top ten?"

He shrugged. "You think, then, if it isn't because you're in the top ten, it would be for one of two other reasons, right? Your parents or whoever is paying your scholarship." He sat forward. "Or is there something else?"

"What would that be? I don't have any information about my parents besides what everyone else already knows. And, I have no idea who my benefactor is." She crossed her arms over her chest. "The idea has merit, but I don't know how to explore it."

They sat for some time in silence until Imogene asked Kade how he'd done. He recounted his own experience with the Trial, finishing with, "I can't believe Dwellen beat Hemsen and me by only a few minutes." He groaned and leaned back in his chair. A few moments later, he added, "I'm glad you're okay, Ima. Gave me a bit of a scare."

She rolled her eyes but smiled. "Yeah. Right."

He shrugged. "Okay. Whatever." He stood. "Believe what you want, Sol."

"I will, Kade."

He grinned at her. "Timaeus. And don't I know it." He stared just a beat longer than he needed to, then gave a quick nod, more to himself than to her. "I better get back for evening protocol. Rather not have clean up duty in the bandon stalls."

She laughed. "Wouldn't want that." She watched him walk from the room wondering what he'd meant earlier, what all that emotion on his face had been saying. Her heart had picked up speed and was still racing as she wondered what he'd wanted to say but hadn't. She focused on trying to get her heart back into place and realized it was getting harder and harder to do so where Timaeus Kade was concerned.

When she finally shuffled into her dorm room, the comfort of the familiar assuaged her. The clean scent of her favorite aromatic pod, the accolades she'd earned situated around the room on her shelves, the pictures she'd collected of her friends that flashed on the hanging screens, the dark plum comforter she'd spent her own credits to buy. She dumped the bag on the floor with a thud and started toward the bed, but something out of place caught her eye.

Sitting on the clear surface of her desk was a small box. She leaned forward to look closer. The wooden box was intricately carved with raised symbols. She pushed it, as if it might release a monster the moment she touched it, but it only slid across the surface of the desk. Scoffing at her ridiculousness, she picked it up. Ten sides. She didn't recognize the symbols, but it was beautiful. Underneath it, on the desktop, the parchment had been smoothed flat and left under the box.

Her heartbeat scrambled as her gaze jumped from the paper to the wooden box, discerning they were connected. She just didn't know how, and it was clear she needed to determine that connection. If she'd learned anything in the last several turns, someone was after her. With the appearance of what seemed dangerously strange gifts—if they had anything to do with it—it was even more imperative to answer: who was behind them?

UNITED FEDERATION OF THE BELLENIUM SYSTEM

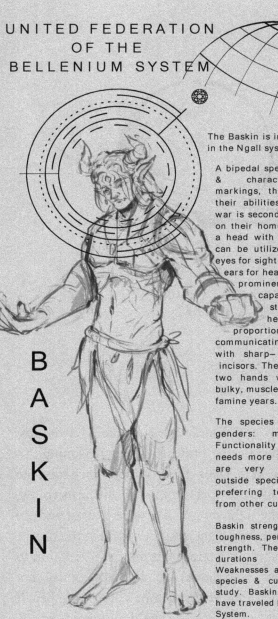

BASKIN

The Baskin is indigenous to Serta in the Ngall system.

A bipedal species with blue skin & characteristic cultural markings, they are known for their abilities in battle, though war is secondary to nomadic life on their home world. They have a head with small horns which can be utilized in defense, two eyes for sight, & small pointy ears for hearing, though their prominent nose with extra capabilities for scent is stronger than their hearing. They have a proportional mouth for communicating, eating, & killing, with sharp— often protruding— incisors. They have two arms & two hands with strong, often bulky, muscle mass necessary for famine years.

The species is born with two genders: male & female. Functionality of this species needs more study. The Baskins are very inhospitable with outside species & antagonistic, preferring to remain solitary from other cultures.

Baskin strengths consist of their toughness, persistence, & physical strength. They can survive long durations without water. Weaknesses are unknown as the species & culture needs further study. Baskin are not known to have traveled beyond the Billenium System.

9

FRIENDS & FEINDS

Imogene's nerves had decided to take over the rest of her body, despite the protests of her reasoning. So when one of the Year Twos dropped their lunch tray, the crash sounded like the opening fire of a sidearm volley. Coupled with the tightening in Imogene's chest and the air trapped in her lungs, she couldn't contain the rage.

She knew she was better than the baser reaction to stress and fear. She should be able to control her reactions, and yet they seemed to be controlling her. It had been almost two turns since she'd returned from the plains, and one from the infirmary. She'd spent a good night sleeping in her own bed.

She should be feeling more like normal, but she wasn't.

Dwellen had attacked her.

Someone had messed with her pack.

Someone could have killed her.

Someone was targeting her.

With her heart banging against the inside of her throat, Imogene stalked across the cafeteria. Everyone in her path skittered out of her way; she knew her face was carting around the next war. When she sat down at her usual place, she smacked the tray a little too hard against the tabletop.

"Whoa. What's what?" Jenna asked. A single golden-brown eyebrow arched over one of her eyes.

Imogene shot her a glare then wilted with an apology. "I'm just so angry," she confessed. "I feel like a mess. How am I supposed to do well in the Trials?"

"You're better than that," Tsua said and sucked up a Wimptyn worm from his broth.

"I don't feel better than that," she admitted.

"Whoever is in on this is counting on doing exactly that," Tsua said. "You off your game makes whatever they're trying to accomplish easier."

At his unusually harsh tone, Imogene looked up from her tray.

"This is it," Tsua continued. "You are in it, and

maybe whatever you're facing is slagged, but this is more real world than any trial will ever give you. Can you hold yourself together to demonstrate you belong or are you going to break?"

Tsua was right, as usual. She needed to pull herself together. She gave him a quick nod, then glanced around the room. Her gaze collided with Kade.

He sat with his friends, his body appearing relaxed as he lounged in his seat, but his features told her a different story. His dark gaze met hers, his features drawn into a frown. At one time, that might have incited her ire, but getting to know him a bit better, she deciphered it as... concern, upending her resolve to keep Kade in the neat box she'd assigned him.

She looked at Vempur, who moved a spoon through his lunch, his mind somewhere else as well. "The next trial is a test of our intellect," he said.

"What do you think it will be?" Imogene asked, though it was more for polite conversation and to keep her mind on something else.

"It's always a game of some sort. Last year's recruits were paired off to face one another for a game of Smuggler's Run." Jenna stabbed a bunch of leafy greens with her utensil.

Imogene imagined the game board, the varied pieces, and the strategy necessary to best an opponent. "The Earth game chess the year before." She pushed her food around on her plate.

"Probably something similar." Tsua slurped another worm.

"Anyone know how opponents are chosen?" Vempur asked.

Everyone shook their heads, but Tsua said, "I would hypothesize our data is run through an algorithm which then assigns partners–" Tsua's thought dropped off into silence when someone said near them, loud enough to get their attention—

"Who loses all the slag in their pack for a trial?"

—followed by a bark of laughter.

Imogene turned in her seat and looked at Dwellen, surrounded by a couple of his lackeys. He was staring at her, a horrible smirk drawing up his upper lip. If Imogene had a no-nonsense relationship with most everyone outside of her friends, Dwellen was a hate-hate relationship. Then again, Dwellen had a hate-hate relationship with most everyone.

Vempur stood. "Was it you? I wouldn't put playing dirty past you, Ridig."

Imogene grasped his thick arm. "Don't," she told him. "He's a waste of time."

Dwellen's eyes narrowed. "You're one to make claims," he said and took a step toward them.

Despite how awful he was, Dwellen was an impressive cadet, tall, muscular, and fit. The broken bones, the horns, the scars, and the inked markings on his body indicative of his Baskin traditions, gave him a threatening presence, and he proved his capabilities in most respects because of his place on the leaderboard.

"Tell me, Sol. You think you have a sun's chance to get a placement outside of Carnos? We all know that's where you belong. Your weak human ass is so easy to push around."

Imogene felt Vempur's arm muscles tense under her hand.

"What the fuck does that mean?" Vempur snapped.

Holding tight to her friend, she replied, "I don't know, Ridig. You think you'll top out over ten on the leaderboard to get a placement outside of bootlicking, ass-sniffing plebe?" She maneuvered her body between them.

It was a dig, given he was always flirting with his placement in the top ten. Her insult hit exactly like it was supposed to, his light blue skin darkening with anger. Everyone knew Dwellen had tutors, and the running underhanded taunt was that he was going to be fortunate to rank out as an officer with grunt duty. It was a ridiculous insult considering he was in the top ten and doing fine academically, but it never failed to get under Dwellen's skin. Besides, he was a mean slag.

He took another step toward her. "Shall we redo the canyon, Sol? Last workout, I went too easy on you. This time I'll make sure you hit bottom."

With a loud shout, Vempur surged toward Dwellen. "I will end you," he said, bodily removing Imogene as an obstacle between them.

"No!" Imogene yelled. "He's not worth it."

"Vempur!" Jenna cried out.

Suddenly Kade was between the two giants, his hand on each of their chests. "Save it for the Trials."

The Globe was silent, all eyes watching the drama unfold. A few halos waited, seeing if they needed to intervene, but this was the Academy. This sort of competition was fed, nurtured, and expected.

Dwellen pushed Kade's hand away but backed up a step. "You're right, Kade." He smirked again, his color returning to normal. Then he scoffed, a thick sound full of malicious intent, and shook his head. "Don't worry, Sol. You'll get what's coming to you." He looked at Vempur, then at Kade. "All of you will." Then he turned and walked away.

"What was that?" Jenna asked from behind Imogene.

Vempur turned and looked at Imogene. "You lied to me." He was furious.

She shook her head. "No."

"Equivocated then."

"I didn't want that to happen." She pointed to where Dwellen had just stood. "I don't want anything happening to you."

"You don't trust me," he said.

"Of course I do," she snapped.

"But not about this."

"About everything," she said and thought of the mystery gifts she hadn't yet shared with him.

Vempur's anger clicked in the back of his throat as he grabbed his things. "Just not about this." He shouldered past her and walked from the room.

Jenna grabbed her stuff. "I'll make sure he's okay."

Imogene watched them both disappear through the doors as the cadets in the cafeteria resumed their ritual. Then she turned and glanced at Kade, whose sudden appearance between Dwellen and Vempur rattled her. She acknowledged they were allies of a tenuous sort, but to step in and willingly help Vempur? That was beyond their treaty. Kade was still acting standoffish, but also attentive in a forced inconspicuous manner. For appearances, she decided, since everyone knew they hated one another and wouldn't mistake them for allies.

She returned to her spot at the table and tried to find peace to eat her meal, but her body wouldn't stop shaking.

"It might be worth taking a closer look at Dwellen," Tsua said as if they were taking a stroll around campus, then slurped another worm.

"I need to find Vempur."

"You should let him calm down," Tsua called after her, but she ignored him and hurried from the Globe.

Despite her best efforts, however, she couldn't find him, and he wasn't answering his Com.

Now in her dorm room after her afternoon classes,

she paced, considering the merits of going to Vempur's room and knocking down the door. Only a knock at her door surprised her.

"Vempur!" she called and opened the door, ready to make amends, but instead of her best friend, it was her commanding officer, Halo Billuk, with another teacher, Halo Nesthamal.

Imogene jumped to attention.

"At ease, Seven," Halo Billuk replied.

"Is everything okay?" She worked through everything she was supposed to do and couldn't think of anything she'd missed. "There's still some time before evening protocol."

"Halo Ripkin has your floor."

Imogene's gut rolled with trepidation instead of the remnants of groff. "Why?"

Halo Billuk glanced at Nesthamal then back at Imogene. "We need you to come with us."

"I'll just grab—"

"Leave it," Nesthamal said, the tone of his voice brooking no argument.

Imogene made sure she had her ID and Com, and left the room, trailing the haloes down the hallway to the lift. "What's happened?" she asked.

Nesthamal directed students to wait for a different lift.

Imogene noted the students' reactions, their assessing looks, their whispers. "Is this about what happened during the trial?"

"No."

She wasn't sure who'd spoken, and without additional information, she just followed. The lift opened to the lobby of the main floor of the dorms, and she followed the two teachers through the courtyard past the Baskin Monolith toward The Sphere, the main offices of all the officials of the Academy.

Eventually, she was taken in through a door to a room she'd never been in, a conference room with a shiny ebony table surrounded by twelve chairs. There were windows facing the courtyard on one side of the room, but the rest of the walls were solid for privacy.

Inside, Sirkuhl Glyn was waiting with the two Fourth Order officers she'd met a few turns prior. Each of them silently watched Imogene walk across the room. Halo Billuk indicated she should sit. She didn't, however, standing behind the chair with her heart racing in her chest.

She felt the need to fill the silence with words but pressed her teeth together, waiting to understand what was happening.

"Please sit, cadet," Glyn said, his voice deep and rumbling. His wide-set dark eyes landed on her, and she felt them drift over her features, assessing, measuring as he frowned.

This wasn't good, whatever it was.

Imogene followed orders and glanced at the Fourth

Order officers across the table from her.

"Sol. Know why you're here?" Officer Mutez—the astra—asked. His eyes were narrowed as he watched her.

She glanced at Glyn. "No, sir."

The Zardish officer—Tynos—tapped on the console, opening an image that floated in the space between them. It looked like a zip-message sent over Com. Imogene leaned forward to read it.

"That's your name at the bottom?"

Imogene's eyes dipped. It was. She looked up. "I didn't write this."

"Is that your name there, at the bottom?" Officer Tynos asked.

"It's a name that looks like mine, but it isn't mine. I've never seen this zip before."

"And the addressee?" Officer Mutez asked.

Jordie. Bartemslow.

Imogene knew the cadet. He was a 4th year legacy on her floor, but she didn't offer that, trepidation building inside her like a wave. "What about him?"

"Is he on your floor?"

"Yes." Imogene refused to offer any more information, a fluttering of nerves and awareness alighting in her gut. Something was off.

"Bartemslow is related to Federation Senator Bartemslow, yes?" Tynos asked.

Imogene shrugged. "Is he?"

Mutez narrowed his eyes. "You didn't know that?"

Imogene did, but an awareness zinged between her gut and the base of her neck, warning her to remain vague. "Should I? Every cadet on my floor is just a cadet."

Tynos tapped the table once more, highlighting the image, then zoomed in closer. "Please read the highlighted portion."

Imogene cleared her throat and looked at the illuminated words highlighted a light gray on the screen. She read, "'A good word with your father, and you'll get prime assignments. If you don't, you know who my mother was, right?'" Imogene sat back in her chair, putting distance between her and the screen.

"Finish it, please," Tynos ordered.

Her eyes jumped between the zip-message and Sirkuhl Glyn, to the officers and back again. "I didn't write that." But she knew how it would look.

"Read it."

Imogene swallowed, then read, "'I can't promise the house of the senate will be safe.'" Shock, confusion, and fear drew her blood away from her face and pooled around her heart, making its beat painful. Her gaze jumped from Tynos, to Mutez, to Glyn. "I didn't write that. I wouldn't."

"And yet it was sent to cadet Bartemslow's Com—from yours."

"That's impossible," Imogene said. "I didn't write

that."

"Impossible? Why?"

"I just wouldn't." Only she knew how flimsy it sounded, how the evidence was stacked against her. "Someone could have hacked my Com–"

Mutez typed something into his Com. "Why?"

Imogene glanced at Glyn. "Sir? I didn't do it."

"We can check the time of the transmission and the source verification for Sol's Com," Sirkuhl Glyn stated. "I'm sure there is an explanation."

"We'll be taking Sol into custody."

"What?" Imogene started and popped up from her chair.

Tynos and Mutez stood. "We have the safety of the senate to consider."

"I didn't write that," Imogene shouted, pointing at the screen.

"Silence," Glyn said, the depth of his Felleen voice reverberating through the room like a rumble of thunder shaking the ground beneath them. "Sit."

Imogene obeyed.

"You will not be taking a student into custody until we have conclusive evidence that proves that student a threat. Until you have more than circumstantial evidence, Sol will return to her duties," Glyn said. "In the meantime, you may continue your investigation–"

"You would interfere with an UFB investigation at the risk of the senate?" Officer Tynos asked.

"And you would question a superior UFB officer?" Glyn rebutted.

Tynos frowned.

"You haven't proven my cadet sent that message," Glyn continued, surprising Imogene. "We exist by an honor code, and the cadet claims it wasn't sent by her. We will operate under our constitutional protocols, even here. That is UFB protocol."

The officers stood, their hard gazes on Imogene's face.

Mutez cleared his throat. "Except the danger of the circumstances are a bit more elevated, don't you think?"

"How so?" Glyn asked.

Mutez looked at her, his eyes boring into hers. "She's a Sol."

"Which means little more than you being an astra, Officer Mutez," Glyn said, his words sounding like hammer falls. He stood, rising to his intimidating height. "The welfare of my cadet is mine. Until you present me with more evidence, Sol is free to attend to her responsibilities here at the Academy. Are we clear?"

The Fourth Order officers acquiesced, despite their obvious reluctance.

"It doesn't need to be said that this is a mark against your placement offer. It's been rescinded," one of them said. Imogene wasn't sure which one. It didn't really matter.

When the door had closed behind them, Imogene

finally looked up at the Sirkuhl. "I didn't–"

"Stand when you address me."

Imogene jumped to her feet, the chair she'd been sitting in slamming against the wall. "Yes, sir."

"I swear to you, Sol. If I discover you had anything to do with this–"

Her eyes jumped to his. "I didn't."

The silence between them stretched a bit too long to be comfortable. Then he offered a tiny, nearly imperceptible nod. "Dismissed."

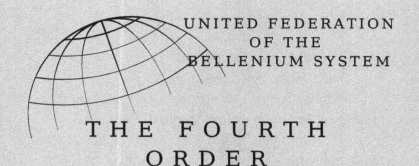

THE FOURTH
ORDER

The Dark War began in 67C3. Then, in 67C8, a massive transit station——Station 452——that served the entire Billenium System shipping & intergalactic travel was bombed. Legion——a terrorist organization ——was responsible for the crime, quelling the dissent. Legion leaders were rounded up, tried by the tribunal, & put to death on Carnos. Support shifted back to the Federation, who rescinded Order 98.53B but instituted incentives for extended contracts. Additional Order 98.53C8a was penned & ratified, which outlawed impressment, as well as Order 98.53C8b, which created the Federation Fourth Order, the Federation law enforcement agency.

A full system agency, this group is responsible for intersystem and interplanetary crime.

10

MAKING PLANS

Vempur had been the first to appear at her door. The moment he'd stepped into her room, he'd wrapped her in a hug.

"I'm so sorry I didn't tell you," she said. "I was just trying to–"

"I know what you were trying to do," Vempur replied. "I don't like it, but I understand it. I would kill for you, and you'd do everything in your power to keep me from it."

"For the record, I do trust you," she said, knowing she needed to tell him about the gifts but hadn't because Jenna arrived, followed by Tsua, and it seemed so irrelevant to the whole of the boiling cauldron of a mess she found herself in.

Then she filled them in on what had happened.

"The Fourth Order rescinded your offer and is investigating you." Vempur repeated her words, his heavy brow collapsed over his completely black eyes. He leaned against the kitchenette counter; his arms crossed over his chest.

Imogene nodded. She was sitting at her desk looking at the wooden box. She reached out and touched it. "I know people don't like me but this—"

"—is next level," Jenna finished, adjusting herself on Imogene's bed. "Who would do something like that?"

Imogene glanced at each of her friends. They looked like she felt, long faces with worried lines etched between their eyes. Since Tsua didn't have prominent eyebrows, his skin swirled deep brown and flashed orange as thoughts moved through his mind.

"There are probably hundreds of students and teachers here who have a motive," she admitted and slumped in her seat, arms crossed over her chest.

"Yes. But this—" Jenna started and paused. "Academy code is rigid. If they're caught, they're out."

"If I can't clear my name, I'm out!" Imogene

exclaimed.

Vempur swore. "Then we have to clear your name. If we can't prove it, then we find out who did it."

Tsua's skin glowed a bright orange. "I have an idea, but it could get us in major trouble if we get caught." His chair hovered in the space at the end of Imogene's bed.

"What is it?"

"You said the email was in the school's system?" he asked.

"The officer pulled it up on the compu-server."

"If we can access the information, I might be able to navigate a workaround to identify the message's origin. It might give us a name."

"Don't you think they already did that? They said it came from my Com."

"Did they say when the message was sent?"

"No."

"It could take a day or two to isolate the correct components in all the scripts to filter it," Tsua said, "so I doubt they'd have it yet."

"Could we just download it from our readers and Coms?" Jenna asked.

"I doubt it's sitting where any student can access it." Tsua replied. "—and if I try to hack it, it will leave a trail. We need to get into the confidential files and download them so we can access them without walls and without leaving digitrails."

"How do we do that?" Imogene asked.

"We have to break into a server access point and download the data."

"Where are they?"

"There are three on campus. One is at the mainframe. That's impossible. Second option is in security. Far more complicated."

"And the third?"

"The Sirkuhl's office."

"Why there?"

"It's the failsafe in case something ever happened at the school. If any of them go down, they have backups."

"Could someone have hacked one of the servers to plant the message?" Vempur asked.

"Plausible," Tsua said, "but it would require the same thing to avoid leaving a trail. The likelihood is miniscule. I think we might be able to find out where it was sent if we get the download."

"How do we do it?" Imogene asked.

Tsua paused, looking around at each of them, then leaned forward. "I'm serious, Imogene. If we take this route and get caught–"

"That's why I'll do it," she said. "No way I'm putting you at risk."

"We stage a distraction to get Sirkuhl Glyn out of his office, and one of us–"

"Me," Imogene interjected.

"You break in and get the download."

"I don't like it," Vempur said, wrapping a hand around his neck.

"You think I should just wait around for Fourth Order to arrest me? I get kicked out of school anyway. At least by doing this," she stopped, realizing her pitch was a little too loud. "At least if I do this, it's in my hands, right?"

Vempur threw out a hand toward her. "But you didn't do it!" His eyes implored her to be reasonable. "It will come out that you didn't do it."

"Unless someone covered their tracks," Tsua said.

"And Imogene Sol is the perfect scapegoat," Jenna added.

They were silent, the buzz of the electronic lights providing a hum around them.

"What's the worse that happens if we wait?" Vempur asked, his eyes on Tsua instead of Imogene.

"Imogene gets charged with a crime and kicked out," Tsua said.

"Gets found guilty and sent to Carnos," Jenna added.

"And if she just gets caught but proves she's innocent?" Vempur asked.

"I get kicked out of school and the best job I can ever get is as a binder on Carnos."

Vempur rubbed the back of his neck with a hand. "And if we get away with it?"

"Imogene's name is cleared, we find the culprit, and

it's business as usual," Tsua replied.

Vempur took a deep breath, then asked, "Is there a possibility that by doing nothing, we could still find out who did it?"

They all looked at each other, pondering the legitimate question. Then Tsua said, "If the culprit didn't cover their tracks, which, given the timing of everything, is a possibility. I mean... for someone to have been able to do this without leaving tracks, they had to break into a server, hack into your Com from the backside, and plant the message. Unless–"

"Unless what?" Imogene asked.

"Unless someone got ahold of your Com? Made a clone?"

"No. I don't think there's been any opportunity." But her eyes slid to the box. There'd been an opportunity to sneak that into her room.

Tsua looked at Vempur. "As precarious as it is, it does seem the best possible scenario to clear Imogene's name."

"Odds for success?" Jenna asked.

Tsua was quiet, his skin swirling orange. "All things considered? I think Imogene has a chance to come out on top if we do this–" —he looked around at each of them— "even if we don't like the means to do it."

"I've already said I'll do anything to clear my name," Imogene said. "Vempur? I could really use you on my side."

He looked at her. "I'm always on your side, Imogene. Always, which is why I'm going to question it. But I will help. If Tsua says this is the right way, I trust him. I mean, you are only the smartest being in our class."

"This is true," Tsua grinned, his sharp teeth bright in his mouth.

Imogene picked up the box. "I need to tell you something," she said, knowing they deserved all the information.

Her friends fell silent, their expressions variations of concern.

She held out the box. "Someone broke into my room and left this on my desk."

Vempur snatched it out of her hand. "What the fuck? Someone broke into your room?" His eyes jumped to hers.

She shuddered, having locked up that little bit of information into a small compartment to ignore it, but saying it out loud made it real. Someone had gotten into her room. Someone had been in her room without her permission. She watched Vempur eye the box.

Jenna inched toward the edge of the bed. "Did they take anything? Get ahold of your Com?"

Imogene shook her head. "My Com is always with me. Just left that—"

"What if it was a bomb or something?"

She hadn't considered that and swallowed. "Well,

it's taking its sweet time to detonate."

"That doesn't look like a bomb," Tsua said. "May I?"

Vempur placed the box in Tsua's outstretched hand.

"You don't know who left it?" Tsua asked.

"If I knew that, maybe we'd be closer to who's actually behind the ruination of my life."

Tsua glanced at her then back at the box. "It looks like a puzzle box." He turned it over in his hands. "Each of these symbols," he pointed at one and then another on the surface, "is probably a part of figuring out how to open it."

"You think there's something in it?" Jenna asked, holding her hand out to see it.

Tsua handed her the box. "Maybe." He turned to look at Imogene, his skin swirling with dark colors. "No clue who gave it to you?"

Imogene shook her head. "I wondered if it was connected to all the other bad stuff."

"Why?" Vempur asked.

She shrugged. "Coincidence, I guess. Timing."

"Maybe getting it open would offer you some insight."

"What if it's boobytrapped," Jenna said. She handed the box to Imogene.

"You have to figure out the symbols, which means you need a cipher," Tsua said.

"Cipher?" Imogene asked.

"Come on. You guys all took code breaking in year five. The code. Unless you find the key, you won't break the code." He cleared his throat. "And currently, we have bigger issues to worry about."

"Except that someone knows how to break into your room, and someone also tried to end you in the last trial," Vempur said, frowning. "I don't like it."

"Right, and Imogene possibly getting kicked out might have to take precedence," Jenna said. "We have to deal with one thing at a time. So, what do we need to do next?" Jenna asked.

"I have a plan," Tsua grinned, his sharp teeth prominently displayed with his smile.

11

HEIST

Slipping away from morning protocol as Sirkuhl Glyn addressed the cadets, Imogene didn't think about what she knew was about to happen as soon as he was done with his morning speech. She might have been trying to keep Vempur from fighting with Dwellen, but now he was going to instigate it as a distraction to give her time.

"I'll cover you on the feeds," Tsua had said. "I'll

just reroute the image so no one can track your movements. As far as anyone is concerned, you'll be at morning protocol."

Imogene inconspicuously removed herself from the room, taking the path they'd planned from the Globe to the Sirkuhl's office. She moved with a purpose, hoping to avoid any other personnel, and for the first time in what felt like a long time, luck seemed to be on her side. When she stepped into the vestibule, Castoring wasn't at his desk, just like Tsua had said.

"He always takes a break during morning protocol."

Imogene moved through the outer room and into the Sirkuhl's inner office.

"You'll need to bring up the files on his desk Com. It will be password protected, but I've got a work around for you. The only problem is, the work around will take some time to find the passcode," Tsua had said.

"Which means," Jenna had added, "you'll have to keep the fight going, Vempur."

He'd looked a bit too gleeful about it, his smile somewhat feral. "Gladly."

"Just don't get kicked out."

"No one gets kicked out for fighting, Sol," Vempur had said.

Now, Imogene pulled up the Com and set the small, round disk Tsua had given her on the top. The Com lit up around the disk as code drifted in neat, binary lines, numbers and symbols shifting until one would catch. "Come on," Imogene muttered.

"Imogene!" someone whisper-yelled at her.

She jumped, pressing a palm against her chest, her heart frozen painfully inside, and stared at Kade, his back against the closed door. She hadn't even heard the door open. "What the hell?" she hissed at him. "Are you, slagging smoke? What are you–"

"What are you doing?" he said.

"What are *you* doing?"

"Following you! You snuck out of protocol."

She swore.

"You're breaking and entering. Come on. You shouldn't be here."

"No, Kade. This is exactly where I need to be. You shouldn't be here. Just turn around and forget what you've seen." Three of the ten symbols had been hacked on the Com.

"I can't."

Imogene straightened. "I swear on Turnus, Kade. Just go!"

"Just tell me why–"

She scoffed. Four symbols. She needed to get him out of here.

"I heard about the Fourth Order pulling their offer," he said.

"Well then, you know why I'm here."

"No. I don't. Not for Fourth Order."

"No. Not for a placement. For my freaking life. Let's just say I've been accused of doing something I didn't do." Five symbols.

"Ima–" He walked across the room.

Six symbols. Four to go.

"What, Kade? What do you want me to say? Someone is screwing with me. I'm just trying to be in control of something here, even if it's fucked up."

He turned her to face him. "I promised to help you."

She searched his face, the depth of his dark eyes looking for the tells, the lies he might be saying with his looks rather than his words. "Well, you getting caught won't help me," she said quietly. "Neither will you getting kicked out on my account. I'm here on my own."

"But now I'm invested," he said. His eyes traced her features.

She shivered and looked back at the disk. Two left.

"Someone framed me threatening the Federation."

"What?!" He jerked back. "How?"

"Fourth Order has a zip from me to one of my cadets—a senator's son—blackmailing him for a favor with his father, with a threat to bomb the senate if he doesn't come through."

"Bomb? What the–"

"Right. It looks like it was sent from my Com, but I swear, Kade, I didn't send it."

"You're here to get a closer look."

Imogene nodded.

The disk flashed, the passcode unlocked, and the Com opened, the golden beams stretched out in three dimensions over the surface.

"Just type your name into the search," Tsua had said when she'd asked what to look for.

Imogene did that now. Every file that contained her name flew up from the desktop into a haphazard stack of computer files. She laid down a second file on the desk's surface and selected the save.

Suddenly, there was a noise at the door.

"Castoring, I need you to contact security." The Sirkuhl's voice. "And I want those boys here, yesterday. My Com alerted me that someone is in my office–"

Kade snatched the disk off the desktop, the golden lines of the desk Com files dissipating like collapsing sand as he grasped Imogene's hand and pulled her into a closet as the outer door opened. He closed the closet door gently; it clicked shut, hiding them inside the cramped space filled with server equipment just as the Sirkuhl stalked past, muttering.

There was barely enough room for one person to stand, let alone two. With Kade's hands pressed against the machinery behind her, Imogene's chest, belly, and thighs were pressed against his. She was too afraid to move, too afraid to disrupt any of the items and alert the Sirkuhl they were there. It wasn't just her now at risk, but Kade with her. She held still, trying to hold her breath as well, but her racing heart prevented it.

Kade dipped his head, his lips against her cheek near her ear. "Relax, Ima," he whispered.

She wanted to snap at him that it was easier said than done, while at the same time chills erupted across her skin, rushing through her, and upending most of her coherent thoughts.

"We'll get out of here," he continued, pressing a touch closer. "I promise."

Her breath caught, her lips near his shoulder, and she was certain he'd heard, his body shifting slightly. She could press her lips to his shoulder but reminded herself she was in no position just then to be thinking such ridiculous thoughts. She tried to adjust but couldn't in the limited space that served to only push them closer.

One of Kade's arms banded around her, keeping her still. "Don't move."

"Sir?" Castoring's voice filtered through the door. "I called security." It sounded far away.

"Where are they?"

"Security said it might be best to interview them at Codex. They have them separated and think putting them back together right now might be too volatile."

"Fine. Why would someone say anyone was here? Office is clear," Sirkuhl Glyn said. There was a silent moment that stretched too long, and Imogene's breath caught, afraid they would be found. In that space, she decided she was a fool—that she should have just trusted things would work out. Only in the next thought, she decided with the exception of getting into the Academy, not much in her life had.

"With me, Castoring," Glyn said, breaking her thoughts. His footsteps moved past the door, then faded. A door shut, followed by another.

After several counts to thirty, followed by one more just to be sure, Imogene asked, "Do you think it's safe?"

"What?"

"Clear to go?"

"Oh. Right," Kade said and opened the door a smidge to look out. "Clear," he said.

"Castoring?"

"Hopefully not at his desk." Kade walked softly— so softly he didn't make a sound—to the door and peered out. "He must have gone with the Sirkuhl. Hurry. Let's go."

Once they were in the hall and walking back toward the Globe, Imogene cleared her throat. "Thank you. Again."

Kade took Imogene's hand and placed the storage disk in her palm. "I told you I'm here to help. Maybe it's time to start trusting me." Then he was gone.

12

TEAM UP

Imogene stopped at the edge of the game fields. With a hand against a shiny dark Mycyte pillar around the perimeter of the Grove, she scanned the crowd of Year Seven ranks for her friends. Each cadet was dressed in their black and white workout uniforms, contrasting with the vibrant green of the grass stretched like a carpet until it met the far boundary of the opposite side of the Mycyte pillar perimeter. The uniforms made it difficult to discern any one from the other. The Game Fields were made up of several spaces for competition, the Grove, the Arena, the Winnow, and the Basin. As cadets, they'd spent a lot of time there training their bodies and their minds for the final Trials and life beyond the Academy.

"Imogene!" Jenna waved. She was stretching out, Tsua and Vempur with her.

Imogene jogged over to them, squelching the disappointment when she didn't see Kade in the crowd, and dropped to the soft loam.

Vempur had a new bruise on his face, which she cataloged with her eyes.

"Don't worry," he said. "You should see Dwellen."

"Were you in trouble?" Tsua asked.

"I got clean-up duty at the Globe," Vempur said.

"Was it worth it?" Jenna asked.

"Absolutely."

Everyone smiled.

"Guess who I ran into," Imogene said.

"Who?" Tsua asked.

"Kade." She shook her head. "He turned out to be a great asset."

"What? How?" The shock on Tsua's face turned his already pale face paler, and the veining of his blood routing to his brain gave him a bluish tinge.

She lowered her voice. "Someone tipped off the

Sirkuhl."

"What?" Vempur's voice hitched a touch higher.

"Who knew?" Jenna asked, looking around. "Besides us?"

"Good question," Imogene said.

"Maybe someone overheard?" Tsua asked.

"How did Kade know?" Vempur asked.

"Yes. Curious." Tsua's skin swirled yellow.

"He followed me." Imogene stretched.

"Maybe someone else saw you leave too? Followed you and alerted Glyn?" Tsua reasoned.

"Nothing to be done for it now. It's done. Kade saved my ass. So tonight?"

"You got it?" Jenna whispered.

Imogene nodded. "I think we should invite Kade."

Vempur shook his dark head. "I don't know." The click in the back of his throat sounded off. "What if he set you up?"

"Then why not turn me in? He could have and didn't. That's important, I think."

"Can we trust him?" Vempur's eyes drooped with concern at the edges, matching the shape of his mouth.

Imogene shrugged. "I'm willing to take the risk if it means figuring this out. Someone is after me, and maybe he'll be able to add a new perspective."

"I say yes," Jenna said.

They stretched in silence, the sounds of other cadets talking, laughing, and getting ready for training around them taking up the space.

"I think it's a good idea." Tsua, not really looking at anyone, nodded. His skin was still swirling.

"Truly?" Vempur's tone was incredulous.

"I am." Tsua's skin shifted blue. "Hear me out. Kade's smart. He's physically strong. He's nearly even with Imogene in all rankings. What is it a differential of what? Seven overall points?"

"He has been helpful," Jenna reminded them.

"And if he's out to get Imogene, wouldn't it be better to keep an eye on him?" Tsua added.

"And if he isn't, he'd be a good ally against whoever is," Jenna said.

Imogene liked that they echoed her thoughts.

"I'll invite him tonight," Imogene said.

"No." Tsua held up his claw, his digits curved with sharp points. "Let Vempur. Better to maintain the norm with you and Kade as perceived enemies. Someone is watching you. They might notice."

Later, Imogene sat in her room listening to Jenna and Tsua argue about how to bring up the information she'd stolen from the Sirkuhl's office on the room's

Com without being caught on the network.

There was a knock at the door, then Vempur stepped through, followed by Kade. The door slid shut once he was inside. Imogene watched him look around, as if cataloging the space. Her space. It made her feel warm.

"Kade," Tsua said, his tone even and revealing nothing.

"We've only got sixty snaps," Kade said, "before Halo Baleen looks for me at lights out."

"Imogene told us you helped her today?"

He nodded, his eyes meeting Imogene's before sliding to the floor. It was a tell, but she wasn't sure what it was telling her. "She filled me in." He stopped and looked around at all of them.

"You're smart," Tsua said and floated across the room in his hover chair. "Truthfully, we're not sure if we can trust you."

Kade's face gave nothing away. "Likewise."

A span of time stretched as they all measured Kade and he them.

"Perfect," Tsua said and turned back to her. "Imogene, what did you get?"

She stood from her cot and drew the flash disk from a pocket of her shirt hanging in the closet, then held it over the desk Com. "Is it encrypted?"

"I got it," Tsua said, taking it from her. He tapped the desk Com, the symbols floating above the surface shifting before he set the disk on the tabletop.

"I have to say," Kade said. "This was fucking ballsy."

"That's our Imogene," Vempur said, but his eyes were boring holes into Kade. "Ballsy."

After Tsua tapped the mechanism, the projection jumped up, filling the space, only this time it was readable rather than just lines of code. "Let's study the incident report, then," Tsua said and looked at the time. "We're down to forty-five snaps."

Thirty minutes later, after going through the zip and the other files pertaining to Imogene, and no closer to a culprit, Vempur sighed and stood. "I don't think there's anything here."

"I agree with Vempur," Kade said. He glanced at Imogene.

"What about Dwellen?" Vempur snapped, his hands rolling into fists at his sides.

She shook her head. "It doesn't track. Dwellen may hate me, but–"

"Dwellen is more interested in what he can accomplish with his fists rather than what he can do with a Com," Tsua observed, his fingers still tapping at the Com.

"What did you hope to find?" Jenna asked, changing the subject.

"I don't know. Maybe something indicating who sent it. But it came from your Com, Imogene," he said, tapping the code. "Right here."

"I didn't write it."

"We know that," Tsua said. "I just mean that whoever sent it was smart enough to get ahold of your Com to do it, or else knew how to hack it on the backside. There are a few people on campus besides me that I know could do it. I could start there," he said.

"It isn't the way you write, Sol," Vempur offered. He pointed out some of the language in the threat. "Who says something like *failure to comply*? Doesn't sound like you."

"Because it wasn't. Why go to the trouble?" she asked Tsua, knowing his mind worked in ways hers couldn't, often seeing a thousand steps ahead to her one or two.

"Can you think of nothing?" he asked.

Imogene ran through all the reasons someone would have it out for her. "The only outlier is my sponsorship to be here and my parents. But again: why?" she asked. "I barely remember them. I was five when it happened. Besides, they were just foot soldiers to a movement."

"You don't know?" Kade asked.

"What am I supposed to know?"

"Do any of you?" He looked around at their faces, then paused and swallowed, as if measuring what he was about to say. "Imogene, the files say your parents weren't just plebe insurgents, they were the leaders of the insurrection during the Dark War." He didn't look up from his hands.

Jenna sat forward on Imogene's bed. "That might make you a very interesting person to the Federation."

"And why you might be threatened with Carnos? Prime placement to keep an eye on you and out of the way in case you share your parents' sympathies." Tsua floated across the room toward the door, so Kade had to move closer to the end of the bed to make room for him.

"I don't share my parents' sympathies," she scoffed, her attention homing in on Kade's word choice. Insurrection. She wasn't sure why it stood out, but it did.

"If they mess up your Trials, they ensure it." Vempur crossed the room and sat down on the bed near Jenna.

"Who is 'they'?" Imogene asked.

Tsua crossed his arms. "Or better yet, frame her for crimes against a fellow student, and one from a very important family, and guarantee her admittance to Carnos as an inmate."

"Are we saying that 'they' might be bigger than just a random culprit here?" Imogene asked.

Silence took the place of any guesses.

She stood and paced in the small space in front of her desk, biting at her thumbnail. "I need to clear my name."

"Yes. We do." Jenna offered her a rope with her words.

"Ten snaps." Vempur said. "I'll go first." He stopped at the door, nearly as tall and wide as the entry.

He paused and turned to look at Imogene. "Com me later." He glanced at Kade, then back at her, offered her a nod, then disappeared through the doorway.

"I know it doesn't need to be said–"—Jenna grabbed her Com and slipped it into her bag, since they were technically studying— "but we have your back." She hugged Imogene, then followed Vempur from the room.

"Okay if I take the disk?" Tsua asked, holding out his hand.

Imogene placed it in his open palm. "You're the only one that can do anything with it."

"I'll see what I can find out." Tsua slipped it onto a pocket and spun his mechanized hoverboard through the doorway.

The door slid shut with a whisper, so only she and Kade remained.

Her heart picked up speed. "About today–"

"You don't need to say it."

"Thank you."

"I said not to say it." He looked down at the floor.

"I do. You didn't have to stay. You did. You didn't have to help me. You could have been caught–"

"I don't care about that, Ima," he said, taking a step closer. "I care about–" But he stopped, leaving the thought unfinished.

Imogene's heart was racing now, her lungs trying to keep up. "What?"

He nodded, his eyes mapping her face. "I hate that

you're in this position." He reached up and pushed a lock of her hair behind her ear, his fingertips lingering against her skin.

"Can we not talk about that?" she asked and shivered. As much as she was grateful for his help, she was equally self-conscious, about having needed it. She turned away from him, picking up the box to engage her hands and mind with something else.

"Ima?"

She tensed at the nickname and glanced at him over her shoulder.

He seemed to want to say something, his dark gaze following her. It was unnerving, and welcome, and... she shook her head to clear it of her idiocy.

They were allies. A team for a common reason. That was it.

"Is that a Rykan puzzle box?" he asked.

She looked down at it, then up at him. "I think so?"

"My dad has one of those."

"Really?"

Kade nodded. "Yes. He used to put messages in it, then have me solve them."

"Do you know how to solve this?"

He tilted his head. "You need the cipher. Then you can decode it." He reached for it. "Look, there's 10–" —he flipped the box around looking at all ten sides— "No. Wait. Nine. See. This one repeats. Something with nine symbols."

He handed it back to her, his finger brushing against hers. Chills raced up her arms.

"You're down to about five snaps to get back to your hall," she said, quietly.

He nodded but didn't move and glanced down at the floor. His hands were shoved into his pockets.

"Was there something else?"

He looked up at her again. "Yeah. There was, but it doesn't matter." He backed away. "I like your room." Then he smiled, lightening the mood. "Tells me a lot about you."

"Like what?" she asked, following him to the door. She found his shift infuriating, because relaxed, smiling, flirty Kade was even more enticing than broody, competitive Kade. "It's just a place to sleep."

At the doorway, he paused. "See you tomorrow."

"I suppose so, Kade." And for the first time, she offered him a smile.

"Timaeus," he replied, then disappeared through the door.

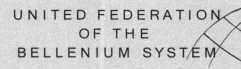

M N E M O N E

The Mnemone is a water species from Hommash I in the Enoz System. They have a large head—the forehead is ridged with echolocation capabilities. The species has two large eyes with a variety of lenses for seeing, a nose with the ability to close for underwater swimming as well as gills that are able to close when out of water. They have a small mouth for eating and killing.

Communication has been learned via vocalization, but most Mnemones use their hands to speak as well as their skin which is translucent & changes color with their emotions & thoughts. They have two arms & two hands, & their lower half consists of a varied number of tentacles, the number of which often denotes age.

The species is born without gender. At approximately 6 years, the gender will form, but it remains unfixed & fluid, able to adapt as necessary to one's mate once selected. Mnemones mate for life.

Mnemone strengths consist of their abilities in water. They are able to breathe & function in an underwater environment & are unparalleled in the water with speed & agility. Weaknesses consist of needing necessary mechanisms to make above water living accessible. This species is intelligent & communicative. Mnemone are not known to have traveled beyond the Billenium System.

13

MOTIVES: UNCLEAR

Imogene waited, though what she was waiting for was a mystery. The other shoe to drop, perhaps? Fourth Order to storm into the classroom and arrest her? A change in the shadow games she was inadvertently playing? The next trial was a half a turn away. Or maybe—surprise, surprise—something good to happen? She wasn't sure anymore. Without anything to help her clear her name, she was just waiting for the inevitable. And maybe that was what the trajectory of her life had always been.

She didn't look up at the group of halos speaking at the front of the room. There were 35 Year Sevens in the room listening to a lecture about credit management. Since classes were over for them now that the Trials had begun, the Academy ushered them into these ridiculous seminars meant to prepare them for the future but just felt like such a waste of time.

"How many of you have received your placements?" Halo Rushesh asked.

Most of the room raised their hands.

Imogene didn't, but Vempur did.

She sat up and looked at him. "What the hell?" she mouthed.

He leaned toward her. "I was going to tell you. After."

Imogene swallowed the lump in her throat, hating that tears filled her eyes. She was happy for Vempur but feeling sorry for herself. And that was a terrible reason to cry. Only she couldn't help herself. She got up and ducked out into the hall, moving quickly for the bathroom to reset herself.

The sounds of a door opening and closing echoed behind her, but she didn't turn to look.

"Imogene?"

She turned to face Vempur, tears trickling down her

face now. "I didn't want you to see," she said like thumps against a punching bag.

Then suddenly his arms were around her, folding her into his hug. His chin rested on the top of her head. "I didn't want to make you feel bad."

"What's with that?" She sobbed, pushing him away. "I'm not glass."

"I know—" He reached for her, but she stepped back. "But look at you."

Imogene pressed her fingers into her eyes. "I feel like a jerk. First Jenna. Now you didn't want to tell me. As if I'd fall apart. And that's sort of what I'm doing, isn't it? Is this who I am? Is that what everyone thinks of me?" She looked at him.

He shook his head. "You're going through a lot—

"And maybe sharing your joy would help!" She turned away from him and started down the hall.

"But you feel bad."

She turned with her arms out to her sides and whisper-yelled, "I feel scared!"

Vempur stumbled and stalled.

She stopped and dropped her arms. "And you— this—makes me feel like things are normal. Good."

Vempur started again. "I'm sorry."

She shook her head. "I'm sorry. I can't escape this stupid name."

Vempur grabbed hold of her, wrapping her back up into his hug, and she relaxed into it.

"I'm sorry for yelling," she said. "What did you get?"

"I get to choose."

"Nice. How many?"

"Two. I got an offer for the Chancellor's security force."

"Wow," she said against his chest, smiling. "Or?"

"I don't want the other one."

She leaned back and searched his face. His teeth were pressed together, but he covered it with a smile. "Fourth Order?" she asked, already knowing.

Vempur cleared his throat and nodded.

She returned to leaning her cheek against his warmth and tightened her arms around him. "You should take the one that makes you most excited."

"Yeah."

After a few more moments, she stepped back and looked up at him. "I'm happy for you."

"I know you are."

"I mean it. Just because things are... the way they are, doesn't mean I'm not happy for you."

"I get it."

"Do you?"

He nodded. "Yeah."

The door opened down the hall, and she glanced over Vempur's shoulder. Kade peeked out at them, stalled for a second, then turned around and went back inside without saying a word.

"Do we have to go back in?" she asked and looked up at Vempur's face.

"Probably." He released her from his hug and took her hand in his.

She dragged her feet as he led her down the hall. "I don't know how much more time I can devote to listening to lectures about budgets when we've already been doing it for years."

"They're checking their boxes, Imogene." He tugged her after him.

She smiled, grateful for Vempur, and suddenly hopeful, though she wasn't sure she had a right to be. As she walked back into the classroom, she held on tightly to it anyway.

But later, alone in her room, she couldn't shake her thoughts. She felt like she was standing at the bottom of a hole looking up without a way out, and she wasn't sure how she'd gotten there. She reached out and fiddled with the unsolvable puzzle box on her desk, wondering again who'd given it to her. Under the pad of her finger the wood of the box was smooth. Pulling it closer, she turned it over, looking at it once more.

"You've missed something, Imogene," she muttered. "Always missing something."

She rubbed a thumb along one of the symbols, which depressed when pressed.

"What's the cipher?" she said aloud as if the box might tell her itself, then turned it over in her hand.

"Ten sides." She tapped each one. "Imogene Sol." 10 letters.

She tapped her desk Com and opened a blank document, where she wrote her name, wondering if it looked like the symbols on the box. There were some similarities, but not enough of any likeness to seem like a viable choice. She set the box on the desktop.

"Analyze symbols," she told the computer.

The desk Com circled the box, the green rings circling the item, analyzing. She could see it thinking, the flashing symbols running through a database. "A rune dialect of Lavish in the Ryken system," the computer's gentle voice stated. "The symbols represent numbers."

"What are they?"

The screen displayed 10 numbers. Two repeated. "Nine numbers," Imogene said, recalling what Kade had said. She looked at her name once more. "Ten letters," she repeated and counted out her name once more, realizing there were only eight unique letters. "So much for that," she said, flicking the box across the desktop.

A knock at her bedroom door interrupted. She turned off the computer before padding across the room in her bare feet.

It was Kade.

"Oh," she said, surprised.

She only ever expected one of her friends, and she supposed Kade was now a friend of sorts, but him showing up at her door uninvited was a first. And goodness if he didn't look good. Dressed in black joggers and a white t-shirt, his already dark hair wavy and darker because it was damp. He looked... unsure, which Imogene thought must be incorrect. She'd never known him to be unsure about anything.

"What are you doing here?" she asked, wondering if someone was watching.

He glanced around. "May I come in before someone sees me?"

"Ashamed to be seen with me?" she asked.

He scowled. "No. Just trying to keep our collaboration under wraps."

She stepped back, a clean scent enveloping her as he walked past. He glanced at her bare feet, then turned his dark-eyed gaze to her body, sliding from her toes to her legs up to her face. Her skin heated as his perusal. While she wasn't overly modest, Kade's study of her in her sleeping clothes—pink shorts and a matching tank—made her feel seen in ways that fluttered her insides and made her interested in drawing him closer.

"I wasn't expecting company." She moved around him, grabbed the navy-blue sweater draped on her desk chair, and slipped into it.

"You don't need to–" He stopped and cleared his throat. "I surprised you. Sorry."

"What do you want?" She flinched at her voice. The clipped tone wasn't what she wanted, but defensive and distant was her norm. Old habits died hard.

His mouth opened, then closed.

She wondered if he was nervous.

"Can I sit?"

She glanced at her desk chair, then pushed it toward him while she sat on her bed.

The color of his cheeks deepened, which suddenly made her feel better, and she couldn't help but smile.

"Are you uncomfortable, Kade?" She'd never seen him so discomfited.

"Timaeus, and a little."

She laughed quietly. It was satisfying to see him outside of his comfort zone. "Is it because I'm in my pajamas?"

His eyes flashed from his hands to her eyes, and the flush crept across his face. She wondered if he'd feel as hot against her fingertips as she imagined.

"No," he sputtered.

She grinned wider and looked down at his shoes. "It totally is. Why? Because you aren't used to seeing me in anything else but fatigues?"

He looked away, his jaw sharpening. "Stop, Ima. There are lots of reasons."

Her smile faded, and she wasn't sure if she should feel insulted. His words said one thing, but when he looked at her again, his eyes said another, his gaze dropping to her mouth.

She didn't want to think about it. She didn't want to

wonder where following that trail might take her, especially knowing how much she wanted to travel it.

"Okay. Sorry. I'm just messing with you. What are you doing here?"

"Tomorrow's trial. It's Kobosham."

Her mouth opened before she asked, "How do you know?"

"One of the halos let it slip. I overheard," he said vaguely. "I wanted you to know. I think you deserve the tip after that last trial." He swiped his palms over his pants. "Are you familiar with the game?"

She nodded. "Yes. I've played it." She was familiar with how to play the strategy game from the Akros System, but she wasn't specifically attuned to the ins and outs of the strategy behind it. This could be disastrous for her. "You?"

He nodded. "I play it a lot with my family. You know that this trial narrows the pool by half?"

She swallowed and nodded, terrified that this was it for her.

"You know the game well enough to win?"

She shrugged, at first because her pride wouldn't let her admit it, but then realized she had more to lose by not being truthful. She sighed. "No."

But she wondered why he would tell her and give her an advantage in the Trials. She hated that she defaulted to the belief that someone wouldn't just help her, out of kindness, but other than Vempur, Jenna, and sometimes Tsua—because Tsua did what needed to be done for Tsua first, and his desire to help her had to do with the fact this happened to be an interesting puzzle to be solved—she hadn't come across many people who would.

Kade bent, moving his body to meet her eyes, which she kept on the white fabric of his shirt. "Do you want to play?"

She met his eyes, which were somehow both hopeful and worried. "Now?" she asked.

He nodded.

Her eyes measured him. "Why are you doing this?"

He stood. "Is it so hard to believe that I like you, Ima?" He walked over to her desk and drew it away from the wall so they could situate themselves on either side. When he pressed the console, a holographic version of the game board appeared on the desk's surface.

She rolled the desk so she could sit on her bed opposite Kade. "Yeah. Actually. We've been adversaries a long time."

"Correction: you've been an adversary for a long time."

Words rose in her throat to argue but then got caught. She examined all the ways they'd interacted over the years, and looking at them through that lens, she could see what he said was true. She was the one who'd kept him at arm's length. The one who'd dressed him as an enemy. He'd never been rude to her, never talked down to her, never indicated she was other than a fierce competitor. She knew she'd done it to protect herself, because if Timaeus Kade wasn't her adversary, that could make him her friend. And if he was her friend, she wasn't sure she could manage her attraction to him as the current moment verified. She worked better the other way because it was safer.

She swallowed and worked her bottom lip with her teeth.

Kade's eyes stalled on her mouth for a beat too long, buzzing the base of her spine and climbing up to her neck. Then he looked away and sat. "Let's play. We'll make sure you know this game as well as I do before I leave.

She sat across from him and smiled. "Thank you, Kade."

"Timaeus." He offered her a brilliant smile, his confidence returning. "Now, tell me what you already know."

She did.

"Okay. Good. At least you've got the rules," he said and set up the board.

"You and your family play?" she asked, watching his hands move across the desk Com with precise movements.

He hummed an affirmation, concentrating. His brows shifted over those dark eyes she'd always loved.

He looked so serious.

"What are they like?"

"My family?" He stopped and looked at her through the three-dimensional hologram of the game. The green lines glowed against his skin. "Great."

"Tell me about them."

He looked back at the console, tapped it, and answered, "There's my dad, my mom, my older brothers Galileo and Penn, and my baby sister, Cairo. Though she's not really a baby. She's a third year."

"Here? At the Ring?"

He nodded. "Make the first move," he said. "Yeah. Here. Where else?"

"I've just never seen you with her."

He grinned, and his smile made her insides pitch and melt. "You and I haven't spent much time together, Ima."

She smiled and followed Kade's first move.

"It's a fact I'd like to rectify," he said, moving a game piece. "What about you? Any siblings."

She shook her head though his statement lingered. But she couldn't stay there, because if she did, it would dredge up too many feelings. Instead, she swiped several of his collected pieces.

"Nice move," Kade said and laid a new piece.

"You can count Vempur. I chose him. As a brother."

Kade's eyes jumped to hers, then to her hand as she made a move. They played in silence for some time

166

aside from Kade offering pointers about different options.

"Do you like it?" she asked.

"What? The game?"

"No. Being a brother."

"It has its pros and cons." He smiled and scooped up a bunch of her pieces. "Like sometimes, Penn and Cairo think they can just take my stuff. Pen because he's older and Cairo because she's the baby. She's always stealing my clothes. But then, sometimes when I need to talk to someone–"—his cheeks flushed, and he stopped moving, looking at the flashing indicator that it was his turn— "it's nice to have someone to talk to for advice. Galileo is great for advice." His eyes drifted to hers and held them.

She looked away first and made her move.

"I win," Kade said and made his move. The screen erupted with fireworks before fading away between them.

"Good job."

"Let's analyze it." He punched some keys on the screen, and the game moves jumped up between them. Kade stood and moved around the desk to sit next to her on the bed, flipping the screen so they could both read it.

Focus on the screen, she told herself, but keeping her mind there proved difficult when his thigh was pressed against the outside of hers. When he pointed, she was thinking about the way his shoulder bumped hers. Every movement offered her another layer of his scent, and she was afraid she might press her nose into his neck and inhale. With him so close, her body was rioting, wanting to grab hold of his face, press him back onto that plum comforter she loved so much, and climb on top of him.

"Ima. Focus."

She blinked, and her cheeks heated. "Sorry."

His eyes drifted over her features, stalling on her lips. "Where were you?"

She opened her mouth to come up with an excuse but couldn't think of a single thing and just repeated her apology.

Kade's eyes jumped from her mouth to her eyes. "You have to focus," he said, but the sound was empty, his hand flattening on the bed behind her hip. He leaned forward.

That organ in her chest slammed up against her ribs with an excited rhythm.

She leaned forward to meet him, hopeful.

The desk Com beeped.

They jolted apart.

Are you still playing? flashed with a beeping countdown to power down.

"Slag," Kade said and stood, putting distance between them, then pressed continue. "The Trial is tomorrow. We have to focus." He cleared his throat and moved sort of haphazardly through the room before putting the desk between them again. "Let's play again."

"Right. Good. Again," she said, wholeheartedly committed to focusing on the game rather than what had almost happened and how much she wouldn't have hated it. She frowned, angry with herself for forgetting her purpose and goals. She had a trial to win.

THE SECOND TRIAL

This is an individual trial that tests one's intellect & mental acuity. The goal is to present remaining cadets with a test challenging their performance under pressure & is often a strategic game played between two cadets. An elimination trial, the trial of Acumen narrows the recruit class by half & provides the winner the opportunity to continue onto the next trial. Those that lose this trial are placed either in prior offered placements or join the Federation as mid-level cadets.

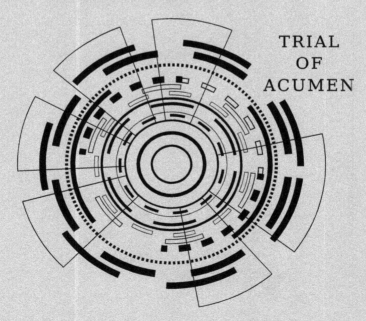

TRIAL OF ACUMEN

14

THE SECOND TRIAL

Imogene—clumped up with Tsua, Jenna, and Vempur—walked into the Codex's main room ready to face the trial. The giant room had floor-to-vaulted-ceiling windows, rare tomes and research materials shelved along the walls, and shiny pillars of black mycyte around its perimeter. The space was set up with individual tables framed with two chairs, a Kobosham game board set up on the center of each table, though the pieces hadn't been distributed yet. No computer version for the Trials. Bright light from the suns filtered through the windows casting the room in a reddish, golden light, the coolant that spilled through the room kept the environment regulated.

"There's the check in," Jenna said and led them to a table where they received their seat placement and a bag filled with their game pieces. They wouldn't know their opponent until they sat down to play at the designated time.

"Kobosham it is then," Tsua glanced around the room.

"I'm really nervous." Imogene looked for Kade.

"Why?" Vempur asked.

"I'm just—" She turned to her friend. "Residual freak-out."

Vempur draped a heavy arm over her shoulders. "Sol, you're going to be fine. This trial won't be life or death."

"But winning it is," she muttered. His arm tightened around her. "What if I get an opponent I can't beat? I'm not great at this game."

"I heard you had some private lessons." Vempur winked at her. "Though I can't say I approve." His smile faded. "He's an arrogant ass."

"What? How?"

"He came to see me first."

"Who?" Jenna asked.

Imogene stumbled on her words until she croaked out, "Why?"

"He said he knew the game, and I guess to make sure it was okay?"

"Who? What?" Jenna asked again.

"Kade," Tsua provided.

"Are you kidding?" Jenna crossed her arms.

"What's that supposed to mean?" Imogene asked Vempur. "Asked? Like for permission?"

"Not kidding." Tsua's claw clacked against his Com as usual.

Jenna sighed. "Oh. That's really sweet."

Vempur looked at Jenna. "Sweet?" He made an irritated noise, refocusing on Imogene. "I still don't like him." He shrugged. "But if you got the help you need, then whatever."

"Permission?" This infuriated her. She glanced around to find Kade. When she did, his back was to her. He was dressed in his gray fatigues like the rest of them, but she couldn't miss him, as if his energy was a homing beacon.

The night before, his teasing, his smile, the easy way they'd worked together over Kobosham wound around her like her comfortable sweater. It was a sweater she wanted to snuggle into and keep, but one she figured was better to get rid of because those feelings would unravel her. They would push her off her game and make her complacent.

And now Vempur was watching her.

"Permission? From you?"

He tensed and frowned. "Don't get upset. I think he was trying to be respectful of our relationship, Sol. He didn't know what–" He stopped.

"He thought you and me… were–" She couldn't say it but her hand flipped back and forth between them.

"I guess."

"You two?" Jenna frowned.

Imogene shook her head. "Sorry. I didn't mean to snap at you," she told Vempur.

Her friend studied her a few extra beats, then leaned closer. "Do you like him, Sol?" He asked this quietly, the tone of his voice weighted with more awareness than Imogene liked. He waited for her answer.

She glanced at Vempur again, who was suddenly too close, his black eyes large and knowing, and though he was like her brother, his face was too curious. The space of the silence stretched between them too long.

In her mind, she thought about playing the game with Kade the night before, the way looking at him had awakened feelings that wiggled like a creature inside of her. How his smile and their banter had made her feel relaxed and secure. How when he'd touched her hand, she'd thought her skin might combust. How those feelings had been happening a lot more lately.

"Are you sure you want to move there?" he'd asked

during one game, a smile in the sound of his voice.

Her gaze had flicked up from the board to his face. "Why?"

He'd smirked. "Well, Ima—" Then he'd proceeded to explain the possible outcomes of that move if she were facing a good opponent, his hands pushing the holographic pieces around.

Frustrated with her ignorance, she'd reached across the board. "Okay. Okay. Your point is made."

Their hands had brushed. This after the almost kiss.

Kade had stilled, then reached for her hand. "Don't be angry." His smirked had faded, his eyes a darker brown.

Her heart had picked up speed, the feel of his hand holding hers shooting bolts of light up her arm, straight to her heart which jolted as if suddenly alive. Then she'd pulled her hand away and made a joke.

Now, she stepped out from under Vempur's heavy arm, away from his knowing gaze, and pushed him. "Why would that be the case?" she asked, though it wasn't just to him but also of herself.

He shrugged again.

When she looked back at Kade, he was now facing her, his eyes locked on her as he watched whatever had just occurred between her and Vempur. He was scowling, but then smirked when he realized she was looking at him.

Arrogant was right.

But perhaps more than that too. Helpful. Thoughtful. Kind. Funny. Things she was only beginning to learn and hated because it meant she couldn't keep him in the enemy category. The frenemy category was dropping away to just the friend. These realizations were dangerous. She couldn't control the slippage of her feelings toward him.

"Welcome to the second trial, cadets." Sirkuhl Glyn's voice interrupted her thoughts, and she reminded herself she needed to focus. "Gather around please."

The 76 Year Sevens—74 had failed to finish the first trial in time—pressed in closer to the Sirkuhl. Their commanding officer waited until they quieted and settled themselves.

"Today, we cull the trial group by half. Win your game and you continue forward. Lose, you are done competing, your scores locked. Please listen closely to the rules, and when directed, proceed to your placement. Good luck and endure."

Halo Grosha stepped forward and explained the rules.

Imogene focused as best she could. She knew she had to do well.

When the halo was done and released them to their spots, all the cadets opened their assignments.

"Good luck," she told her friends and started across the room.

Tsua hovered near her.

Imogene looked at him. "What's your seat number?"

"17."

Imogene slowed. "I'm 18." She glanced at Tsua, then stopped at the table. Her heart sank. "We're playing one another?"

Tsua was staring at the table, confused. "But–"

"It doesn't make sense," she said. "You said they'd pair based on abilities and strengths. You should be playing someone ranked higher, academically."

His brain was swirling. "Or someone messed around with the placements." His shrewd eyes flashed about for the culprit, but there wasn't anyone about.

"I can't beat you, Tsua," she said.

He made a sweeping gesture with his hands and moved his chair into position. "Well, Sol, that's exactly what your enemy is hoping."

She sat. Her emotions upended.

Tsua leveled her with one of his measuring gazes, his relaxed blue flowing back under his skin. "Let's not give whoever it is any satisfaction of freaking out. We'll play our best games, yes?"

Imogene, who felt tears smarting in her eyes, followed Tsua's lead by setting up her side of the board, the movement a way to keep the tears in check. Each game consisted of a board with several variations of blocks, ten stones for each opponent, slots for placement, and a collection zone. The object was to move the stones across the board and collect that opponent's pieces to drop into the collection space. The open slots were safety zones, and the blocks were for strategic placement and steals, but each colored stone and block place had different rules for engagement.

"Imogene."

She looked at her friend over the board.

Tsua smiled, his tiny, sharp teeth showing in his mouth. "Let's play."

She knew she couldn't beat him. He was leagues ahead of everyone academically. She would never be able to beat him at a game of strategy. Ever. Sure, she was smart too, and intellectually bright, but Tsua was a force. She supposed, however, that this was the way it should be—her elimination. She wasn't supposed to be here anyway. The fact that she'd made it this far was a gift.

She nodded at him. "Yes."

He reached out and placed his hand over hers. "Let's not worry about the outcome, okay?"

She wanted to say it was easy for him to be so nonchalant about it, but she didn't. Tsua was her friend, so she nodded again. "Let's just have fun."

He rolled the bones to determine who went first.

Imogene made her move, recalling Kade's lessons about best opening moves.

And so it went, the two of them taking turns until the first game was done. Tsua won, though to Imogene's surprise it had been a narrow victory by only two pieces.

They set up the second game board. Rolled the bones. Tsua started this time. They played. Imogene watched Tsua thinking. He was working the moves in his mind, and she was sure seeing the possibilities of varied outcomes. When he made a move that surprised her—a move that opened his game to possible defeat—she glanced at him, but he maintained his gaze on the board, focused, his blood swirling blue. She analyzed her possible moves, each of them favorable for her. She calculated her best option and took it. Four moves later, she beat him.

"That was a good game," he said. "Challenging."

Her eyes narrowed, but she didn't say anything, wondering if he'd thrown the game but having no proof. She also knew Tsua. He didn't willingly lose anything, fiercely competitive especially when it came to his gift for intellect. "Good game," she said.

His eyes rose to hers. He offered her a smile. "Ready for the final game? Winner takes all?"

She nodded as she replaced her pieces.

They rolled the bones.

Tsua won the toss again and made the first move.

Around the room, other games were finishing up, their victors shaking hands with their opponents. Some were crying. Those with less honor, like Dwellen, crowing their prowess. She thought about Dwellen's threat: *You'll get what's coming to you.* Could Dwellen have somehow rigged the opponents? Could he have been behind the things missing from her pack?

But as much as she tried to fit him into that neat box, he didn't fit. Dwellen crowing over his win, hitting her from behind, blustering in the cafeteria, being an ass for everyone to see, those things made sense. The methodical, underhanded maneuvers didn't. Whoever was after her was doing it in secret, underhanded, messing with other people's Trials.

She thought of the box.

Then the slip of parchment with the word: Surrection.

Watching Tsua make his move, she realized surrection was a ten-letter word. With a repeated letter. Nine letters. Her muscles tensed.

My father gave me a box like this. My family likes puzzles.

Could it be Kade?

Her heartbeat faltered inside her chest considering it. Hating the possibility and knowing her own confirmation bias would keep her from suspecting him.

"Your move, Imogene," Tsua said.

She offered him a smile and a nod, then chastised herself to focus. Even if Tsua walked away with the victory, she needed to give him a competitive game.

Move.

Countermove.

Move.

Countermove.

Both looked for the upper hand.

Tsua studied the board, the time between moves stretching as strategy became even more important. Beneath his skin, his thoughts showed in swirls of color, not that anyone would know what those thoughts entailed, only that they were occurring.

Imogene waited for him to make his move and noticed that a small contingent was beginning to form around them. She studied the board, considering Tsua's possible moves as she thought about what Kade had helped her with the night before.

Would Kade help her then put her with Tsua just so she'd lose?

Tsua made a move.

Her eyes flew up to him with a question, knowing the move he'd made wasn't his best choice.

He wasn't looking at her but kept his eyes on the board.

She wondered if those watching them could see what she was seeing, but she kept going. She pondered her possible moves, and, after determining which was the best, took it.

Move.

Countermove.

As she studied the gameboard, the outcome appeared in her mind as if she were sitting across from Kade in her room. This was her last move. Her victory.

She glanced at Tsua, who's eyes remained on the board, but then snapped up to her face as she set the game piece in its final place and collected the spoils.

She'd won the series. She'd continue in the Trials.

Tsua was done.

Her eyes filled with tears.

Tsua looked up at her and smiled, swirling blue-green.

But she couldn't return the smile.

After shaking his hand, because that was protocol, she pushed away from the table and left the room, trying to hold back her tears.

A few minutes after she reached her room, Jenna called from the other side of the door, "Imogene. Open up."

She complied, the door sliding open to reveal her friends' faces as she swiped at her tears, hating her weakness.

Tsua steered in his chair and swiveled around, forcing Imogene to move. "Why didn't you stay? To celebrate. It was noticed."

"You let me win," she told him. "How could I celebrate eliminating you?"

"Let you? I don't let anyone do anything with respect to me. You know I'm severely competitive, Imogene. You won. Fair and square."

Imogene could feel Jenna and Vempur standing behind her, but her focus was on Tsua. She didn't believe him. "I'll confess to the Sirkuhl."

"Confess what?"

"That you should have won."

"Did you cheat?"

"No."

"Neither did I." He sighed. "Imogene, look, I don't need to win the Trials. Regardless of the outcome, my placement with ComTech is set. I don't need to continue."

"But," Jenna said, "if your seat and opponent was tampered with, it wasn't fair to begin with. For either of you."

"But if we go to the Sirkuhl–"

"No!" The force of Tsua's tone shocked them all into silence. He shook his head, and his body swirled with reddish orange. "Imogene is where she needs to be. Besides, if we do—go to the Sirkuhl—it could influence whatever the culprit is planning. We need things to be business as usual." He looked at Imogene. "Someone wants you out of the Trials. Someone is messing with your placement, so whether I made a dumb decision in Kobosham is irrelevant."

Imogene tilted her head. "Twice?"

He smiled, and his skin flushed purple. "I refuse to comment on mistakes I make. It doesn't reflect well on my intellect."

"I owe you, Tsua," she said quietly, still ashamed it had come to this.

"You do." He grinned at her. "But what are friends for? And true friends don't make other friends wait to eat." He smiled at her.

She smiled back and nodded. But she couldn't shake the feeling that now that she'd won this trial, everything about her rank now made her a fraud.

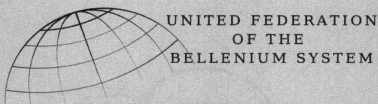

THE THIRD TRIAL

While most of the Academy is structured to commend individual goals & performance, the Federation seeks cadets with the ability to work with others. This trial forces cadets into a partnership that tests their ability to problem solve with another cadet, while still showcasing their physicality, endurance, & fortitude. This elimination trial culls the cadet class to the top ten. Cadets eliminated by this trial are often recruited to high-level placements within the Federation.

TRIAL OF TENACITY

15

THE THIRD TRIAL

Imogene's nerves were fraught with tension, her shoulders so tight she could feel it in her jaw as she entered the Grove a few days later for the third trial. The weight of all that had happened, in addition to knowing Tsua was no longer in the Trials because of her, made it feel like she was dragging around several extra bags. Sirkuhl Glyn's threat—if it had been one—had been hard enough to stomach, but it had only been about her.

Added to the rest, if she didn't do well, what would all of it and Tsua's sacrifice have been for?

She hadn't seen much of Kade over the last several turns beyond shared seminars and workouts. He was keeping his distance, which made her wonder if it was a confirmation of his guilt. She'd passed the second trial. Or was it something else? The one thing she couldn't reconcile, if he were guilty, was why he'd go out of his way to help her. And though there was circumstantial evidence that might point the finger at him, the actual evidence was him being helpful. Just like he said.

She also hadn't had any luck figuring out how to plug in the word as symbols. Aside from the one identifiable symbol because it repeated, figuring out how the others factored was more complicated. And that was if it was the right word though her gut-check told her it was.

She stopped in at the check to register but couldn't do much more than grimace and answer with one-word responses.

"Hold out your arm," the feminine gillick told Imogene, their mottled purple skin smooth. Imogene did, and the gillick used a reader to register her information. "Here's your number." Six. Her rank unchanged after the last trial. They attached the black cuff to Imogene's wrist. "This is so your location is registered during the trial at all times."

A safety precaution for this physical trial. She

wondered if this was a new addition after what had happened to her in the first trial.

"My partner?" Imogene asked.

"Meet at the course." They looked down at their Com. "Number five. The cuff should vibrate to make the connection."

Imogene closed her eyes. Dwellen's last rank had been fifth. "Thanks," she said and turned back to the crowd. If the rankings were the same, she'd be paired with Dwellen.

Slag.

She moved through the crowd and into the thirty-two remaining cadets to find her place and deal with her anxiety about having Dwellen as a partner. She wasn't exactly sure, but if the standings remained, it was likely. A good partner could be the difference between finishing or elimination, and the latter she couldn't afford. But if it was Dwellen, neither could he, which she had going for her.

With the fear of someone sabotaging her, she couldn't help but wonder if perhaps someone might fix this race too, handicap her with a weaker partner. If she thought about it too much, it made her feel like her lungs would come out through her mouth.

She took a deep breath and wove her way through the crowd at the far edge of the Grove. She couldn't afford to let her fears keep her from focusing on the present.

"Imogene!"

Jenna waved.

Imogene took a deeper breath of relief. She hadn't gone to breakfast that morning, needing time to settle her mind and mentally prepare. Vempur stood next to Jenna. Their cuffs were tethered.

"Wow. Did you expect this?" Imogene nodded at their wrists.

"Standings, I guess," Vempur said, drawing up his arm. Jenna's followed.

"Whoa. Remember we're connected," she said. "Who's your partner?"

Imogene shrugged. "I don't know yet, but if I've calculated the standings correctly, it should be Dwellen."

Vempur growled. "I don't like that. Especially after what happened."

"Except he has a lot to lose too if we don't do well. He doesn't have his placement yet either."

Vempur didn't look relieved by that.

"I should probably go find him," she said. "Have you seen Kade yet?"

Jenna shook her head. "Not yet, but good luck kicking his ass."

Imogene smiled. "Yeah. I'll need it."

She continued through the Grove until she heard her name and turned, thinking Vempur was calling her back. He wasn't. It was Kade jogging across the field toward her. She wanted to roll her eyes at how fantastic he looked. The clean lines in their black uniform hugged every curve and line of his body, his wide shoulders and chest, his tapered waist, and muscular arms and legs all contoured by the slick fabric. She suppressed a groan. Fighting his attraction was becoming futile.

He could be trying to ruin you, she reminded herself.

"Kade," she greeted him.

"Timaeus," he corrected, then assessed her as he walked the last few steps to her. "You look–" But he didn't finish. He just smiled.

His perusal made her feel warm, and she knew he'd be able to see her blush, so she turned her head away to pretend to look for her partner.

"Where were you at breakfast?" he asked. "I looked for you."

He'd looked for her?

She glanced back at him. "I checked in with my cadets and returned to my quarters for some visualization exercises."

"Needed some time to think about me then, Ima?" Kade stopped in front of her, his grin infuriating. He stepped closer. "What were you visualizing?"

"Beating you, today." She offered him a flirty smile, then scolded herself for flirting. *Focus, Imogene.*

Her wrist buzzed.

She looked down and watched the tether cord leave her cuff, snap, and connect to the matching cord of

Kade's cuff.

Her eyes flashed from her cuff to his, her mouth open in surprise. "What? I thought–"

His eyes were just as wide. "What the Carnos?"

"–it would be Dwellen," she finished. "Did you do this?" An irrational surge fear spiked inside of her as she thought about racing next to him, but despite her misgivings and doubts, his cooperation had only provided positive evidence of him being truthful and trustworthy. Unless she was completely jaded, his partnership seemed the best possibility. He was physically strong, mentally strong, and he claimed to be her ally.

He shook his head and scowled. "You seem to think I have these magical powers with the administration and a snitchy relationship with those officials. What the Carnos, Ima?"

"Why would we be paired?" Her heart was pounding against the inside of her chest with... she wasn't exactly sure. It didn't feel like fear or anxiety. She wasn't upset to be paired with him, even if it surprised her. The beating of her heart felt—good. "I should have been with Dwellen."

"Well, you're not." He tested the tether and yanked her toward him. She jerked forward but caught herself. "Not bad." He looked around. "I don't know, but it's smart."

"Because we're enemies?"

"Exactly. Come on. Let's see who the competition is. See who Dwellen got placed with." Kade started moving through the crowd all but dragging her, but then stopped for her to catch up.

"If we're partnered, he might be with Sylar." Imogene fell into step with him.

"Or Lon."

Side by side they closed the distance between where they were and the section they'd been assigned. Their predictions were almost perfect.

Kade turned to Imogene and pulled her closer.

She resisted.

"This is the best-case scenario," he said.

"Why?" Unable to fight his pull, she stepped closer.

"Because we can win. You and I, together."

"You think this was tampering?"

He shrugged. "Who cares?" He smiled, one that reached his eyes.

She looked away, because looking at him continued to mess with her insides. "If it was, it seems very poorly thought out." She assessed the other pairs. They all seemed perfectly matched in ability.

"Maybe so." Kade looked around. "If people knew the nature of our relationship had changed, but most everyone assumes we hate one another." He looked at her once more and grinned, wiggling his thick eyebrows. "That would make it sort of genius if we did."

"For the record, until about 20 turns ago, I did hate

you." She smiled to temper the statement.

He crossed his arms, drawing her arm up as he did so. "Hate is a very strong word, Ima."

"This isn't very comfortable." Her arm hung in the space between them, tethered to his. "The other partners don't hate one another," she said, looking around at the other pairs.

Her disdain for Kade had always been loud and public—he was right. Everyone knew. "For the record, I don't hate you."

She couldn't help but look at him then. He was mapping her face with his eyes.

Unsure what to say, she looked away, not sure she could say anything regardless.

"Ima?"

Her eyes met his brown eyes again. Thanks to the tether, they were standing so close she noticed the traces of bright copper in his eyes.

He leaned toward her, and her hand had nowhere to go but to flatten against his arm.

Her heart palpitated in her chest as she tried to keep breathing normal. He was so close. She could turn her face and touch her lips to his skin if she were so inclined. She remained still.

"I'm glad you don't hate me anymore," he said near her ear.

She cleared her throat. "I'm sure that could be remedied."

He chuckled and uncrossed his arms so her hand returned to her side. She knew she should be relieved, but disappointment seemed so much stronger.

The first signal rang about the perimeter of the Grove, indicating it was time to take their marks. Tethered, they made their way to the starting point. A halo introduced the partner race. Time would translate to points and be added to their totals, adjusting the rankings. The Top Ten in rankings would advance to the final trial.

"Together?" Kade asked.

She gave him a quick nod. "Together."

"The 38 of you are the elite," Sirkuhl Glyn said from the dais near the starting line. "Top in your class." His deep voice reverberated from the volume enhancer he spoke through. Dressed in his usual uniform, its brass accents gleaming in the suns' light, his eyes scanned the crowd of students and halos. It was a beautiful day in the shadow of Turnus. "Of the original 180 cadets in your class at the beginning of year one, you have risen to the top of the ranks." He paused, letting that sink in.

Imogene shifted on her feet, her arm drawing Kade with her. She'd forgotten they were tethered. "Sorry," she mouthed.

He smiled.

She refocused on the Sirkuhl once more, trying to calm the haphazard beating of her heart.

"Each of the Trials thus far have tested your mettle in some way. The next trial is no exception. But unlike the first Trials, which tapped into your perseverance, endurance, and intellect, today will add the layer of teamwork. Here at the Ring Academy, we push you to excel on your individuality, and yet the Federation doesn't function on individuality. It is a series of teams serving our inter-galactic treaty. Each of you has a role to play within that broader team. So today, your trial has paired you with another cadet."

Imogene glanced at Kade again. He was looking down at her.

Nerves danced up her spine as she looked back at the commanding officer addressing them.

"Upon arrival, each of you received an assignment which you will open at the sounding buzzer. You've also been given a team survival bag. Please take a moment to open it now and assure it has been filled with the required equipment."

Imogene's lungs tightened, then expanded knowing that Glyn was doing it because of what had happened to her. She wasn't sure what to think of it, the feeling moving through her akin to care and concern, which didn't compute when it came to the commander but was beginning to.

Glancing at Kade, she watched as he opened the bag, beckoning her to look inside with him. Together they cataloged the contents against the list the commanding officer provided. A map, a temporary dwelling, two insulators, a temp light, and rations. Kade zipped the pack and slung the bag onto his back.

"You have exactly three turns to solve your assignment and cross the finish line. Your individual scores will be calculated for final placement in the final trial, but keep in mind that you're still completing this trial as a team. It is in your best interest to finish early, as it will impact your overall total, but you must cross together. The top twenty on the leaderboard will be moving onto the final trial. Do not be comfortable with your current placement," he warned. "This challenge could change everything."

"Three turns?" Imogene looked at Kade.

His brows were raised over his dark eyes.

"If there are any questions, please flag your closest halo in their yellow referee jackets," Sirkuhl Glyn added. "Do not open your assignment until the starting bell rings momentarily or you will be disqualified. Good luck and endure."

Three days? Imogene glanced down at the tether. Three days tied to Timaeus Kade, her nemesis who'd somehow become her ally. Her heart tightened in her chest, then dropped into her gut rolling with nervous anxiety. Hating him, competing with him, tapping into anger were all ways she knew she could cope with her attraction to Kade. Being his friend was so new and added to her attraction. This was untenable.

She closed her eyes. Took a deep breath and reminded herself she had to focus. This set-back couldn't be one. She didn't have the choice but to do well, and with those reminders carefully pinned to her inner psyche, she opened her eyes and looked at Kade.

He was having a hard time meeting her gaze, looking everywhere else but at her. She watched him close his eyes, take a deep breath, and when he opened them, he turned to her with a smile. "Are we ready?" he asked.

The starting bell rang, keeping her from having to answer or to analyze his reaction. She tore open her assignment, the rest of the cadets doing the same around her. She read hers while Kade read his, scanning the words, then rereading them.

The Baskin villages are uprising, angered about the Federations tax increase over water. The Federation is sending orders to Outpost 43. You have been tasked with retrieving the message at headquarters and then delivering it. Good luck and endure.

"What's it say?" she asked him. She hoped they would have the same assignment but knew it was unlikely. This was about teamwork, and what better way to test it than to make the trial more difficult. Imogene figured every single one of the teams had two assignments that needed completing, meaning each of them had to defer to the other at some point.

Kade was pulling off the backpack. "Mine says I need to go to Outpost 21 to get a secret missive for Federation to Outpost 1." He dropped to his knees and laid out the map on the ground—a map of A'mor. It was easy to see where the Academy was on the map, the Cliffs of Mnor, the Marken Plains—real places. Then, marked on the map were fictitious places like Outpost 21 or 43 or HQ.

"Mine is HQ and 43." Imogene traced her finger between the places on the map. They were completely opposite of Kade's. Looking up, she saw they weren't the only team crouched in the grass of the Grove looking at their map. "The best thing to do, I think, would be to set a route that includes all the stops."

Kade was nodding. "The question is, which would be the quickest route?"

Imogene noticed some different markings. "But." She tapped one that existed between Outpost 21 and 43. "What are these?"

Kade looked closer. "There are a bunch of them. Obstacles? Maybe they're keyed in our reader?"

Imogene pulled it out of the bag and looked for the appropriate file, tapping on the symbol. "You're right," she said. "That one is the Baskin uprising. That could cost us time and points."

"Right," he said. "Let's make a plan."

16

NEW PERSPECTIVE

Their initial plan was shot.

Imogene and Kade had their backs pressed against the wall outside of the training grounds at an entrance point she hadn't even known existed that Kade had led them to. It was a narrow opening that looked like it had once been part of the wall but had since crumbled. Tall, unruly grass surrounded them, obscuring them and the opening from anyone who might wander past.

Despite their best attempt at making a plan that would keep them on track to avoid the pitfalls of obstacles, they'd realized they couldn't avoid them all, forced to pick and choose to manage their overall score. Their current predicament had them hiding outside of a freezone, a lawless area rife with corruption and danger—danger to their trial time anyway. They had the choice to skirt around it, adding time but keeping them moving. Or they could take the shortcut through the zone, which could put them ahead, but if caught would tack on penalties and impact their time.

They'd spent the last few minutes arguing.

"I promise, Ima," Kade said.

"You sure?" she asked Kade, who insisted cutting through the zone was the best option. Trusting him was so tentative, she'd had to remind herself they were on the same team. "I hate waiting. I feel like I should be doing something."

He turned his head to look at her, then adjusted his large body so he was sitting instead of squatting. "I know… but going around is going to be just as dangerous, especially in the light of day. If we wait for darkness, we can skirt through the freezone using the shadows. Once we're through, we'll make camp for the night, and it will be easy going to the first outpost for our first mission."

She nodded and mentally filed that he'd called the

task theirs rather than just hers or his, then ignored the warmth of it in the center of her chest. "Right."

"Patience, then?"

She nodded.

"It's hard for you?"

"You noticed?"

He grinned. "I notice a lot of things about you, Sol." He held her eyes a moment before his gaze skittered away.

Her heart skipped in her chest, and she looked out at the landscape, the shadows between the buildings of the Ring Academy stretching as night approached. She wasn't sure how she felt about that admission, or even how to interpret it. So she didn't, reminding herself that they were just allies for now.

"How did you know this spot was here?" she asked.

"My brothers. They gave me the inside information on lots of stuff. Penn–"

"Your middle brother?"

He grinned. "Yes. He loves to find the work around for everything. 'Work smarter, not harder' he's always saying."

"And he shared them?"

"Are you always competing, Sol?"

"I–" Defensiveness rose like a wave.

He chuckled. "I'm just messing with you."

Her heart knocked against her ribs, almost painfully as it worked to slow down and couldn't seem to find the appropriate rhythm.

"How come you've never liked me?" Kade asked, stepping over her silence and getting right to the heart of the matter.

"That isn't true," she said.

"You admitted to hating me."

"I like you fine." Which was a lie. She liked him more than fine, which was a dangerous proposition at the Academy, for her at least. It wasn't like there weren't hookups or people coupling up, but she couldn't let down her guard. Kade made her want to.

He looked at her again, his dark eyes skimming across her features. "You don't need to lie, Sol. Not to me."

She swallowed, unsure what to say, her heart still racing. How did she admit keeping him at arm's length felt safer, otherwise her crush on him would have crushed her? She said, "I can't afford to forget."

"Forget what?"

"The notoriety of my name. Where I come from."

He looked away and adjusted again next to her, stretching out his long legs, his shoulder, his arm, the back of his hand pressing against hers. The heat of that touch slid underneath her skin, slipping between those nerve endings straight to her heart and shifting her internal organs until she didn't recognize where they were located inside her.

"And where is that?" he asked.

"You know–"

"We all know the story," he said. "That's not what I mean." He turned those dark eyes on her again, and she had the sensation he could see through her. See through her words, her excuses, her actions, her defenses. She knew he wasn't asking about her parents or about the event that made her an orphan. He was asking her to go deeper, to share.

She hated it.

"No one will let you forget that," he said, "But that isn't who you are, Ima."

Aside from her friends, she wasn't sure that anyone had ever pushed to know her beyond her backstory. Someone learned who her parents were, and somehow, she stepped into a costume made from the shrapnel they'd left behind. Kade asking felt like he was peeling away her defensive layers.

She felt herself frown at him. "That is all that matters to most."

"Not to me," he said and looked away, giving her a chance to breathe. "I'd like to get to know you." He looked at her again. "Here. I'll tell you something about me, and you share something about you."

She didn't like it, knowing she had too much to lose getting to know him better. Only she wanted that nugget of information like she wanted to win this trial. She nodded.

"What do you want to know?"

She sat down next to him and made herself comfortable, sighing as she did. "Let's see," she said, drawing out the two words into a lengthy sentence, smiling as she did.

He just grinned, his face slightly turned and tilted so he was looking down at her.

"Why did you wait until our final year to offer your help?"

It was his turn to sigh, and he looked away, staring out at the landscape. "I don't–"

"Nope. You want an answer, answer it."

"Give a guy a chance." He smiled, but it faded. "When we were in our first year, at fifteen, I was dumb."

"Only at fifteen?"

"Don't be a smart ass."

She smiled and looked out at the landscape. "That's not an answer."

"I know. I'm not finished, but you're being a smart ass."

"Sorry."

He looked at her with one of those smiles that tugged on her insides. "My father sent me to the Ring with an assignment."

"Assignment?"

"Yeah. He's like that. Ring proud and all."

She knew he came from a Legacy family at the Academy, a family whose lineage stretched back and back to the origin of the formation of the academies back when the Billenium Federation was established, and the academies were designated.

"Then you kicked my ass and everyone else's most of the time. I had to focus extra hard just to try and keep my place. I was also guilty of putting you into the box everyone else did. I was so jealous."

"Jealous?" Imogene couldn't believe that. She'd been jealous of him.

"I can only speak for myself, but yeah. You made it look easy."

"It wasn't. Hasn't been."

"I know that. At 22."

"I thought you made it look easy. That you had it easy."

"But now we both know the truth—how hard we have to work."

It hurt to hear him admit it even though that had always been the assumption. "What changed?"

He plucked a length of tall grass and started twirling it, focused on it instead of her. "My eyes were opened. If I had to work hard, you were putting in two times the—"

"Ten times."

He laughed softly. "Five times more work. When I saw what Mins did—in that spar session—after you'd already bested four opponents, I knew Dwellen would volunteer. I knew he'd pick hand-to-hand after you were already tired, and that he wouldn't hold back. And I couldn't stand by anymore. I'm ashamed it took me so long."

"You took it easy on me?"

"That's what you get from that speech?"

There was something he wasn't saying, but she couldn't figure out what, couldn't read between any of the lines he'd given her because what he had said spoke so loudly. "And now?"

He took a moment, then turned to connect. "I admire you more."

Imogene's breath caught even though the rest of her was racing. Her skin ignited. She looked away, severing eye contact, but doing very little to squelch the rest of the avalanche sensation rushing inside her and burying all her defense mechanisms.

"My turn," he said. "Tell me something you haven't shared with anyone."

She swallowed, wanting to back away from the conversation, afraid of revealing anything to anyone. But a deal was a deal, so she took a deep breath. "When I was five, I lived in an RF on Slegmas Four."

"RF?"

"Replacement Facility." When Kade looked confused, she added, "A home for orphans and rehomed kids. There was this little shop down the street from the facility that carried a variety of goods for the neighborhood that my group's house sister would take us to once a week for a treat. I couldn't get anything—

not usually—and didn't always go, but that day the home mistress told me I'd been given a whole credit to use. That wasn't something I'd ever had before, so I was excited.

"We made the walk to the store. When we got there, I remember walking each aisle with intention, knowing that what I got needed to be special." She glanced at him and saw he was looking at a blade of grass he'd plucked from the ground, twirling it between his fingers. "I knew that I probably wouldn't get to do it ever again. I narrowed the choice down to this pack of glass marbles."

"Marbles?"

"Marbles." She held up her hand and made a circle with her thumb and forefinger. "Glass globes, like mini planets you can hold in your hand."

"Is that why you wanted them?"

Imogene blushed and nodded.

"I don't think I've ever seen one," Kade admitted.

"They were beautiful. Glassy and shiny, all different sorts of colors. Anyway, the bag was just shy of a credit. I carried around my treasure until everyone else was ready, and when everyone had chosen their treasures, we followed the house sister up to the proprietor who calculated the cost. He rang it up but when our sister went to pay, we were exactly a credit short."

Imogene paused for a moment, her throat tightening at the memory. How everyone had looked at her, and how small and insignificant she'd felt. The way the sister had, crouched down, smiled, and said, "You won't miss it right, Imogene?" because Imogene never got to get anything. She cleared her throat, looked up at Kade, and offered a smile. "Well, I didn't get the marbles."

"What? Why?" he asked, frowning.

"We were a credit short."

"Right. But someone else had spent more. Or maybe someone wasn't supposed to get anything. Why were you the one who had to sacrifice?"

She figured her silence was enough affirmation.

"You've always been the one to sacrifice."

"What happened with my parents has always mattered," she finally said, though Kade hadn't ever made her feel like it had. "Remembering it keeps me sharp and competitive. Everyone's made it clear they won't forget, so I have to be the best to prove them wrong."

His expression turned pliable and gentle. "Someone had to move the placement for us to be paired."

She'd thought of it already. "Maybe whoever is trying to sabotage me thought we'd spend the trial fighting."

He chuffed a short laugh. "You, maybe."

Her animosity—she was beginning to see—had been mostly one-sided.

"I'm relieved it wasn't Dwellen," she said.

"After what happened at the workout and the other

day, me too," he replied, his eyes homing in on hers once more before drifting to assess the landscape.

Imogene didn't want to think about his statement and the way it made her feel, afraid, perhaps, she was misunderstanding his meaning. She ignored it, dismissed the buoyant way her body felt momentarily as if in zero gravity, flipping the switch to keep her feet firmly fixed in reality. She longed to say more, but couldn't, so she didn't.

The final rays of Argos dipped behind Turnus casting the land into darkness.

"Ready?" she asked.

Kade was already getting to his feet. "Born ready," he said.

She took a deep breath and followed him through the opening in the wall.

17

TETHERED

The trick was moving together. The tether made it nearly impossible to do anything in sync without the other. Turning, adjusting, switching from lead to follow required a dance. Somehow, though, working with Kade was easier than she anticipated, as if all the years they'd spent at the Academy together competing had sharpened their skills to know the other one so thoroughly. That thought continued to unsettle Imogene, just as sitting with him and talking had, but she couldn't stay in it, not as they worked to complete this important trial.

The training grounds marked as a freezone on their map had been constructed to look like a village one might encounter in the United Federation of the Billenium System. Buildings, shadowed alcoves, clotheslines, abandoned items, and a plethora of hidden spaces teemed with people. A festival was taking place, which worked in their favor, allowing them to avoid the yellow-jacketed referees who would tag them with penalties.

Blots of darkness stretched around them as Imogene followed Kade. He stopped, peeked around the corner of a building, then lurched backward until his back pressed against the outside of one of the perimeter buildings.

"Yellow jacket ahead," he whispered.

With a nod and a simultaneous tug on the tether, Imogene suggested going around the other side.

Kade followed.

She wasn't ready to admit that she liked working with Kade, but since he'd stuck up for her with Dwellen, and since the last two Trials, from preparing for the Kobosham to now working in concert with him, that frightening awareness was burrowing under her skin. She ignored it and led him around the other side of the building. Together, they paused, checking the alleyway for any yellow-jacketed referees, then scurried to the next building, repeating this around the perimeter of the village until they reached the point they needed to cut across at the heart of the village, where Imogene stopped leading and waited.

A quick assessment at the village square revealed it was also the heart of the festival, people milling about as notes of music drifted their way. She could see the hint of lights strung across the alleyway at the square's entrance, hear voices, and see colorful movement beyond their hiding spot.

She glanced at Kade crouched behind her with a clump of colorful fabric wadded up in his arms. "Any suggestions?"

"One," he said, looking down at their tether, then looking up to meet her gaze. "Can I ask you not to get angry?" he asked and grinned.

"Why?"

He smiled and pulled on the short tether, rolling it around his wrist and drawing her toward him. When she was close enough, he linked their hands, sliding his fingers through hers. "I'd like to take you to the festival," he said with a grin, like they weren't actively competing in a trial where all would be lost if she messed this up.

The heat of their joined hands sparked a trail across her skin, igniting a roaring blaze between her shoulder blades. She yanked her hand out of his grasp. "Are you kidding?"

"No." His grin deepened, and she noted the appearance of dimples cut into his cheeks. "Hide in plain sight."

"We'll get tagged."

He lifted the wad of cloth. "No. We'll use these. And the only ones that can tag us are the yellow jackets. We just want to avoid any local plants who can complicate things."

"So we just walk right into the party and pretend like we belong?"

He nodded and unfurled the fabric, clothing he'd obviously pulled off the clothesline they'd passed. Smart. "Put this on. Should fit over your uniform."

She shrugged into it. "It doesn't work," she snapped, unable to pull it over the shared tether.

Kade stepped closer, rewinding the tether around his wrist. "The key will be standing close enough to hide it."

She scooted back.

"Stay still," he said quietly. "I won't bite." Then he finished winding the tether line. "I know we'll be close, but I don't mind." He smiled, adjusting the fabric over her shoulder to her hand in his, then laying fabric over their joined hands. "Okay?"

Though she acknowledged this was doing more to her than it should, she knew it was the right course. "Alright."

They stood close, their arms and legs bumping as they finished putting on the clothing and adding fuel to the flames inside Imogene working their way around from her back to her chest.

"Promise you won't bite?" he asked and held out his hand for her to take once more.

Imogene looked from his face to his open hand. She felt her cheeks heat and hated it, so she said, "I will never make a promise not to bite."

His eyebrows arched over his eyes, and his lips parted.

She took his hand as if to prove to herself she could be unaffected by him. It was a stupid lie.

Kade cleared his throat. "Ready to go to the festival?" The warmth of his breath drifted over the skin of her neck.

She nodded, unable to say anything.

With her hand in Kade's, she followed his lead. He walked from the alleyway, pulling her with him, as he brought them right into the middle of the revelry. People moved in pods around them, some talking and laughing, some drinking, some dancing. Kade pushed in through the crowd as if they belonged there.

When he stopped, Imogene bumped into his back. He turned and pulled her closer, one of his hands burning the skin at her hip.

"A yellow jacket," he whispered. "See her?"

She skimmed the crowd over his shoulder, looking

for the pop of the referee's black and yellow jacket in the chaos of color around them. The sea of people parted, giving a glimpse of the referee a hundred paces in the direction they needed to go.

"I see."

"Maybe she'll move," Kade said. He wrapped his free arm around her, pulled her closer, and began to sway. The warmth of his hand in hers and the other on her back burned through the layers of cloth right into her skin.

"What are you doing?" she asked, figuring she should step away, but did what she wanted and stepped closer. She wanted to look at him, to take stock of his expression, but didn't take her eyes from the yellow jacket.

"Blending in," he whispered, his mouth brushing her cheek. He tucked their tethered hands between them.

Her heart snapped to attention, then lurched forward into a sprint as they danced together just like everyone around them. She thought about all the places her body touched his. The heat localized points spreading and connecting inside her until all she became was a flashpoint.

A part of her wanted to disconnect, afraid to experience the feeling, to know what she'd be missing, but the part of her that longed for connection, imagined an alternative life where she could want this. She had permission, after all. Kade had offered it, and he didn't seem adverse, his hand bunching up the fabric at her back into his fist as he moved closer.

Someone bumped into them from one side, another from the other, jostling them in the chaos of the dancing, which pushed them closer together.

His thighs skimmed against hers. His hips moved; a supple movement that made her stomach dance a discordant rhythm from the rest of her body. Her hand and his were pressed between them, tucked together between their hearts, and she could swear she could feel the racing of Kade's. His hand relaxed at her back, then pressed her closer as his head dipped, his warmth of his breath caressing her skin.

"Is she gone?" he asked, his lips grazing her cheek.

Imogene tightened her grip in his. Her other hand slid across his shoulder, down his arm, her fingers curling around the muscle of his arm.

She looked for the yellow jacket, who seemed to have disappeared. "I don't see her."

It took a moment longer than necessary for either of them to step away, but Imogene did first, keeping hold of his hand and drawing him through the crowd. When they reached the shadows on the other side of the square, they shrugged from their borrowed garments, lengthened the tether, and set out for the perimeter. But rather than a hole in the wall, it was a gate out into the plains watched by another yellow jacket.

Kade swore and slumped against the wall.

Imogene watched the yellow jacket check his communicator.

"What now?" Kade asked.

"I bet they rotate," she said.

"Why?"

"The yellow jacket in the square didn't hold her position. And rotation is what I'd do to keep them awake," she said and pressed her back against the wall next to Kade. "Let's give him a few minutes and see what happens."

Ten minutes later, the yellow jacket walked away, leaving the gate clear.

"Hurry," Imogene said, shoving Kade. "The next one won't be far behind."

They darted across the road, dropping into the darkness of the overhanging trees and up against the gate.

"Shit!" Imogene said when she reached it, looking over her shoulder at Kade. "It's locked."

"Leave it to me," he said, and pulled a small pouch from his pocket. He unzipped it and removed something she couldn't see in the dark. "Keep watch." Lifting the lock, he went to work on the mechanism, inserting the tool into the key port.

Imogene looked out at the roadway, sure that they only had a few minutes before the next yellow jacket appeared. Her gaze darted around the dark. A shadow in the distance stretched toward them. "Hurry," she whispered, pressing up closer to Kade's back. "Someone's coming."

She heard something click.

"Got it."

With a clank and a squeal, Kade pushed open the gate and yanked her through, closing it behind them just as footsteps echoed across the roadway. Kade pulled her out of sight, crouched in the shadows on the other side of the gate, then laid down in the tall grass.

Imogene flattened out next to him.

The footsteps stopped. The sound of a communicator beeped, and a voice asked, "Did you leave the gate unlocked?"

A disembodied voice cracked over the mechanism. "Didn't touch it. Maybe a different rotation?"

"Locking."

There was a click, followed by silence but for the intermittent footfalls of the yellow jacket standing guard just inside the gate. After fifteen minutes, the referee walked away.

Imogene released a breath.

Kade squeezed her hand.

She hadn't even realized they'd been holding hands, and rather than pull away, she squeezed him back.

"Let's go. We'll make camp."

18

WAKING UP

When Imogene opened her eyes, it was still dark, and though she felt like she'd slept, she wasn't sure what time it was. The slick sheen of dark green fabric surrounding her fluttered, indicating a soft breeze outside. A weight was heavy on her hip, a large, warm barrier pressed up against her back.

Timaeus Kade!

She shifted, and the weight on her hip moved, his

arm wrapping around her waist and pulling her closer, nesting her body into the grooves and curves of his. She froze, afraid to wake him up. Not because she was afraid of him, or of being this close, but because she wanted to just allow herself this small sliver of normal. Like dancing.

Shutting her eyes, she imagined this could be real— not part of a trial—and ignored every squawking reminder in her head telling her it wasn't. She could pretend. Just for a moment.

She released a slow breath, her heart racing.

The night before, after getting through the village and the locked gate unscathed, they'd been on a high. They'd followed their plan and map to the first night camp making a fire and setting up the sleeper habitat. She hadn't commented on the size of the tent they had to share. Neither had Kade.

After a quick nibble on their nutrient bars and taking care of their bathroom needs—still tethered but thankfully with enough room to pretend they had privacy—they'd crawled into the sleeper. Due to Kade's width, lying side-by-side had proven difficult, so they'd situated themselves back to front with space between them.

Sleep had claimed her rather quickly.

Now, a sound beyond the sleeper made her eyes fly open once more.

She tensed, listening.

Kade's arm tightened around her. He leaned closer. "Don't move," he whispered.

"Yellow jacket?" she asked.

Based on the rules, they couldn't be penalized for sleeping, but if they got caught beyond the sleeper, they could get tagged.

"Not sure, but I'd rather not check and get hit."

She understood. "Is everything inside?" she asked, thinking about their supplies and if they could be stolen.

Timaeus reached up and tapped the bag in the gear loft above them. "We're good."

"Can you see out the vent?" she asked.

"Not without rolling on top of you and letting whoever is walking through our camp know we're awake."

Her cheeks heated at the thought of Kade rolling on top of her. She squeezed her thighs together and frowned, angry with herself for even allowing the thought to impact her. She'd spent the last several years able to compartmentalize her crush on him, but it was becoming increasingly more difficult. Especially now that they were spending so much time together.

Silence settled around them, and except for her own measured breath mingling with Kade's, there wasn't much to discern beyond the tent.

"Did you mean what you said?" His voice was soft and sultry in her ear.

"About what? We should check–"

He was quiet as she turned, untangling the tether as she did.

"I'll turn onto my stomach and crawl to the vent."

"About biting." He said this quietly, a strange lilt to his tone she was familiar with.

She froze, her eyes jumping to his. "What?" She breathed the word more than said it, then imagined kissing him, pressing her lips to his, then capturing his bottom lip between her teeth. Her heart clacked behind her ribs. She could almost feel her mouth, her lips, her tongue, her teeth exploring every inch of Kade's skin.

She blinked, righting her mind, and her cheeks heated.

And as if he'd been in the same fantasy, he mumbled, "Sorry for asking. Disregard. Uh..." He paused to clear his throat. "Yeah. Check."

She rolled to settle the bouncing of her heart that seemed to be full of helium now and needing to get outside of her chest. Kade's hand rested on the small of her back, and as she inched forward, she wondered when he would lift his hand as her butt inched toward his touch. The departure of his contact was disappointing, but necessary. She hated that she missed it. Refocusing on what was important, she drew the vent flap up slowly, hopeful someone wasn't lingering beyond the confines of their habitat.

There was something there, only it wasn't a yellow jacket. She relaxed, her forehead to the habitat floor.

"It's a bitbit." The cute, gray mammal with gigantic, twitching ears nibbled on a plant outside the tent.

Kade let out a breath mixed with a short laugh. "Of course it is. Should have thought of that."

Imogene rose onto her hands and knees and backed up, returning to her place to glance at Kade. He hadn't quite rolled to his back—the habitat was too small—but enough so that he was looking up at her.

His eyes dipped to her lips before darting away. "We better get a look at the map and review our plan."

"Right," she said and turned as best she could to unfasten the entrance.

Once outside, after another session of tethered morning routine, Imogene found herself bent over the map laid across the ground as they ate their nutrient bars and rehydrated.

Kade pointed to an invisible path they needed to tread between their current position and the first point. "It should be a straight shot."

"Hypothetically." She pointed to a designated marker for the canyon. "This is a problem though."

"Hiding spots?"

She nodded and chewed her bite. "I know it will add time but cutting through there risks getting tagged."

Kade was quiet, pondering, then he looked up, the prism of his dark gaze drawing her in and holding her. She liked how he waited, contemplated things, and thought them through for the best outcome. But he'd also proven adept on the fly too, grabbing the clothes, the dancing, picking the lock. There were so many different facets to him; she was more curious, more intrigued the more she got to know him.

She dragged her gaze away.

"You're right," he said. "The time we'd save will probably get tapped by tags. If we hustle around this–" he pointed to the Cintel Plateau– "we might be able to shave off some time."

She nodded. "Sounds like we're ready then."

They packed up the habitat and set out.

Hour two from the camp, they had effectively skirted the opening of the canyon and picked up the pace. Rather than walk, they ran which didn't leave much room for talking and left Imogene too much time to think. She studied the landscape, grasslands stretching out in all directions around them, though she knew the Cliffs of Mnor rose behind them. They were running the Marken plains, the Lopah Mountain range with its sharp, snowy peaks purple in the distance. The first checkpoint wasn't much further, nestled on the other side of the Ribbon—a river that cut through the plains and created the Cintel Canyon. They just had to get to the other side.

"We have to plan for the bridge," Imogene said as she ran slightly behind Kade.

He glanced over his shoulder to say something. As he did, she caught a glint out of the corner of her eye.

She stopped, yanked on the tether, and dropped just as a marker whizzed past.

"Dammit," she panted.

"What the hell, Imogene. How the slag did you see that?" Kade asked, rolling to his belly next to her. "Where are they?"

"Settled up on the plateau," she said. "The glimmer." She searched for the obscura tech camouflaging the yellow jacket having only caught it out of the corner of her eye. It was a miracle, really.

"I didn't think they could use that tech," Kade muttered. He dug through the bag when the grass and dirt exploded in a succession of pops around them.

"We're pinned down." Imogene curled around herself, then felt the weight of Kade over the top of her. "Are they using live rounds?" she yelled.

"What the fuck?" he asked. "We're in trouble here." He withdrew ocular glass from the bag and held it up. "I see the shimmer, but not who's behind it.

"Should we backtrack to the canyon?"

Kade rolled to his back and handed her the glass. "We should get out of range. They must be using a Federation-Grade Class R weapon."

She didn't know how he knew that, but accepted it, nonetheless, looking from the glass to him.

He turned his head and looked at her. "That's not a yellow jacket, Ima."

She looked back at the plateau through the glass, the

shimmer gone as two forms ran across the edge. "Someone's up there."

Kade rolled back and took the offered glass. With an adjustment, he sucked in a breath. "That's Hemsen and Ravi."

"They were shooting at us?"

Kade looked at her. "That doesn't make sense. How? First, they'd have to have known our location."

"Someone could feed it to them using our location beacons."

"Okay. And the weapon?"

"Someone leaves it for them."

"Then that would mean they'd dumped it for someone to pick up. But why? Why involve more people in this… whatever it is?"

"Should we see if we can find it?"

He was quiet for a moment, contemplating. "I think we have two options. First option, we go after the weapon—if it's there—but it will add time."

"But it could clear my name. Prove that someone is after me."

"Yes, but what if that is the intention, to get you off track and pull you from the trial. We don't place in the top ten, you're out."

Imogene sighed and looked at the plateau. "Second option?"

"We go forward as planned. Report it at the station. They can go after the gun."

"What if the yellows are in on it?"

"It's a risk, but my gut tells me that isn't the case."

She looked back at him.

"I'm willing to do whatever you want, Ima. It's your call."

He was giving her the choice and his support.

Taking a deep breath, she glanced at the sky, watching a few clouds glide past. She waited a few beats, pondering the choice, wondering what to do. She'd spent so much time at the Academy watching her own back, it felt strange to have someone watching it with her.

And that's when she knew she trusted him completely. She also realized this wasn't only her Trial. Lifting her hand, the tether pulled on Kade. She followed the line between them and knew she couldn't sabotage this—not for either of them.

"We keep going. Forward."

He nodded. "Let's get out of range, then we'll run."

"I don't think they're there anymore—the obscura is gone."

"Just in case. I don't want anything happening to you."

"To either of us."

"Right. Yes."

They stayed low and out of sight in the grass, and once it was safe, started off on their run once more, hoping to regain some time. The bridge was clear, which seemed strange to them both, but they crossed without incident, checked in for the first task, and reported the shooting.

"That can't be right," the referee looked at them like they were telling stories. It was Halo Mins, dressed in his yellow-jacket attire.

"About 20 klicks from the bridge across the edge of the plateau," Kade said.

"There aren't any live rounds in this exercise," Mins said. His gaze assessed them, jumping to the tether.

"Well, sir, that doesn't mean that isn't the case," Kade added.

Imogene didn't say anything, knowing full well that she had never been a favorite of Mins and wouldn't start.

The halo pulled out his Com. "I'll make a report."

Imogene was sure it was due to Kade's reporting rather than hers. It certainly helped to be a legacy, and she knew her legacy wasn't the kind Mins appreciated.

"Keep going?" Kade asked.

"Keep going."

19

STUPID FEELINGS

"I've been thinking," Kade said, interrupting Imogene's own contemplation.

She glanced from the small campfire to his face, catching the dance of the fire against his brown skin. His dark eyes were shiny black orbs, glittering in the firelight.

"I don't think it was Hemsen and Ravi."

"Because of the tech?" She'd already considered it.

He nodded and poked at the fire with a stick. "Unless someone else provided them with the obscura tech and that weapon, there's no way they had it."

"And who has that kind of tech?"

He hesitated, his eyes jumping to her.

She understood. Once it was said, it couldn't be unsaid.

"The Federation is the only group I'm aware of that does. Unless fringe groups–"

"Fringe groups?"

His eyes slid from her face back to the fire. "Not everyone is happy in the Federation."

She knew it, but she hadn't pondered it much. It hurt too much considering what her parents had done, who they were to the Federation. The Dark War was a blight on Federation history, and now knowing her parents were figureheads rather than just instruments of the uprising—it felt dangerous rather than just shameful.

"But targeting you doesn't make any sense… sorry, Ima."

"It's okay. I've been saying the same thing. Targeting me would mean someone high up the chain makes a call, right? That's illogical. It must be someone close to home, someone with a personal stake. But this tech…"

"Fourth Order?" he asked.

She'd played with the scenario in her head too. "They have been on campus because of that stupid threat I didn't even make…" She stopped, her throat closing around the harsh words.

Kade didn't reply.

There wasn't a need to.

Instead, they sat in silence. Silence followed them through the rest of the routine, until they were settled in the habitat for the night. Kade was behind her with Imogene slightly turned toward him to accommodate their tether.

She shivered.

"Are you cold?" Kade asked.

"No," she replied, but shivered again as tears sliced against the back of her eyes like little knives. She knew it was the adrenalin, the fear, her emotions tangled up in an unmanageable knot lingering at the center of her chest.

"Ima?"

She hummed through the tremor that sliced through her body.

"May I touch you?"

Under other circumstances, she would have said no, but the weight of what could have happened out on that field, the fact that just by being with her had put Kade in danger, the pressure of having to succeed in Trials that seemed so small in comparison to what she was actually fighting for—it was all too much. That her efforts might not even matter, considering the most powerful entity in the system might be after her was a boulder she couldn't hold up on her own.

But he was offering his support. So she said, "yes," and another tremor rocked through her.

Kade shifted—like he had earlier that morning when all she'd been worried about was a bitbit outside the habitat—and pulled her against him, her body conforming to fit into the contours of his. Strong arms wrapped around and entwined with hers, holding her securely in his embrace.

Then she realized she'd made a mistake.

With her fortitude suddenly in the hands of someone else, she couldn't find the means to hold herself together. Kade's arms were doing it, rather than her own. Her breath caught on a sob, and she gasped. Tears sliced through her defenses and fell.

Kade's arms tightened. "I've got you, Ima," he whispered. "I've got you."

His words were meant to be a land mass, a means of support on which to find firm ground, and she completely collapsed, clinging to that promise.

Since waking, Imogene had felt awkward about the release of her emotional dam. The torrent of regret about that raging flood had carried her through the morning and into their first mission. She was still treading its current as she ran with Kade toward the finish line. As they'd raced across the plains, all she'd had to do was think. She'd spent most of the morning cringing at her outburst and how inept she'd been at acknowledging her emotion.

"I'm sorry about last night," she'd told him as they'd set out from their camp on the final leg of their trial.

"That isn't something to apologize for," Kade had answered, his warm gaze finding hers.

She hadn't allowed herself the comfort of falling into its warmth, instead looking ahead as they'd walked. "Well—" She hadn't known what to say in the glaring light of her vulnerability. It wasn't as if she'd never cried. Of course she had, in the safety of solitude.

"Ima, you were shot at—"

"We were."

He'd ignored her and continued. "Your Trials have been tampered with. You've been accused of something you haven't done. In your shoes, I'd have lost it a long time ago."

She wished she'd thought of something witty or lighthearted to lighten his statements, but all she'd been able to come up with was, "Thanks for... yeah."

"Thanks are also unnecessary. What are friends

for?"

She'd glanced at him, but he hadn't been looking at her and was instead studying the ground. Done with the awkwardness of it, she'd figured it was time to focus on what was ahead and said, "Let's finish this trial."

He'd looked up then and grinned. "Yes. Let's give them something to remember."

So they'd finished. Moved across the terrain working together, skirting the dangers, avoiding yellow jackets until they'd collected what they needed for Kade.

Now, they were nearing the entrance to the grove. The hum of sound could be heard as they cleared the final rise. In the distance, the pillars extending above the outer wall gleamed in the afternoon rays of the suns. Behind the wall, over a thousand young cadets of the Ring Academy were lined up in the Grove—she knew because she'd once been them.

"Think anyone else has crossed?" she asked.

Kade smiled. "Who cares. We're about to. Ready?"

"I was born ready."

They ran the last leg and moved through the arched gateway. A cheer went up loud and cacophonous. Imogene doubted any of that was for her, but Kade was certainly a favorite. As they crossed the finish line, their tether disconnected with a snap, returning them to their independence. Exhausted and grateful, she threw her arms around Kade's neck. "We did it!" She smiled and pressed a cheek to his shoulder.

Kade wrapped his arms around her. "Not a single penalty. That has to be a record!"

She could feel his strength pressed against her ribs, the pressure of his arms at the small of her back. The wall of his chest, the sturdiness of his thighs, the width of his hands holding her against him. Heat burned through her when she realized the direction of her thoughts and how easily she'd dropped her guard. She stepped back to attempt to correct her thoughts. "Good job, partner."

He offered her a tentative smile, one that didn't quite reach his eyes. "Yeah... partner." Then his smile strengthened as he looked over her shoulder. "Cairo."

Imogene turned around at the same time a younger cadet squealed and launched herself at Kade. His sister.

"First!" Cairo exclaimed. "Daddy is going to love it."

Kade grinned at her and adjusted, letting go of Cairo as he turned. "This is Imogene."

She resembled Kade, with those intense dark eyes and gentle features engaging Imogene's gaze. Cairo's dark hair was pulled away from her face in a soft, messy bun. She wasn't in uniform, since being at the Grove as a spectator to the Trials it wasn't required. Her gaze swept across Imogene, who couldn't tell if the young woman was antagonistic or curious. "So this is the famous Imogene Sol."

"Famous?"

Kade elbowed his sister, his skin darkening. "Forgive my sister. She speaks before she thinks." He gave her a look that made Imogene feel both dismissed and vulnerable, assuming he meant Cairo was speaking about Imogene's parents. Whatever it meant, she felt left out.

"Nothing to forgive. Nice to meet you, Cairo." She took a step away. "Enjoy your family," she told Kade.

"Don't go," he said and offered his sister a goodbye. Cairo melted back into the erupting crowd as Hemsen and Ravi crossed. "We should go celebrate."

"What?" Imogene yelled over the din.

Kade grabbed her arm and leaned toward her. "We should go celebrate."

"Well done, cadets," a voice interrupted.

"Sirkuhl," Kade saluted.

Imogene acknowledged her superior as well.

"Impressive." Their commanding officer looked at the Com in his hands. "Not a single penalty." His brows arched over his eyes. "I can't remember that happening in... well, it's been many trial cycles." His eyes jumped to Imogene. "Excellent showing, Sol. Keep up the good work. You too, Kade. I must say, when I saw you two were paired, I did pause."

Imogene gritted her teeth, wary about what their commanding officer would say.

"Sir?" Kade asked.

"Just a surprise. I thought you might drown one another when you got to the Ribbon."

"Or get shot at with live rounds?" Kade frowned.

The Sirkuhl's brow dropped heavily over his eyes. "What are you talking about, cadet?"

"On the plains, near the Cintel Plateau. Obscura tech, a Federation-Grade Class R. We reported it to Halo Min when we checked in," Kade provided.

Sirkuhl's eyes jumped to Imogene's. "Obscura tech?" the commanding officer asked.

"Yes, sir," Imogene confirmed.

Kade and the Sirkuhl exchanged a glance, and tiny hairs on the back of Imogene's neck prickled, though she didn't understand the look that passed between them.

"I will look into it," Sirkuhl Glyn said with a nod. "Dismissed."

Imogene watched him walk away with quick, determined steps toward Hemsen and Ravi. She backed away from Kade.

"Where are you going?" He grasped her arm to keep her there before she was beyond his reach. "Ready to celebrate? While we wait for the others to finish."

She tilted her head and narrowed her eyes. "What was that?" she asked.

"What?"

"Something happened between you and the Sirkuhl. Just then."

His face scrunched up. "What are you talking about?" He shook his head.

"Don't do that to me." She turned away, but he didn't let go of her arm.

Instead, he started walking, pulling her along with him.

"What the Carnos, Kade?" She yanked her arm out of his grasp, and he let her go, stopping to face her.

"Stars, Ima." He swore. "It's Timaeus. And I don't want to risk you running before we can talk about what you just said."

"Just ask."

"May we talk, please?"

She consented with a nod and followed where he led.

They walked past the pillars in silence, followed the walkway past the athletic complex, down the steps toward the center of campus where the Baskin Monolith stood surrounded by rolling hills and trees. Kade led her into a mall surrounded by a trellis covered with greenery and milsk blossoms where there were benches and a semblance of privacy.

He stopped, sighed, and ran a hand through his dark hair as he turned on her. "You don't have to do that." He was frustrated.

"I don't have to do what? Say when I notice something off?"

"There's nothing–" But he stopped, skimming her

features with his gaze, before looking away and shaking his head. "You're right. I'm sorry. And I can see why it would feel like that."

"Like there's stuff happening around here that involves me that I'm left out of? I wonder why I might jump to those conclusions."

"But you don't have to do that, Ima."

"Do what?" She couldn't remember ever seeing him so upset, even with a loss to her at some competition—not since they were younger anyway. Usually, he took it in stride.

"Jump to conclusions about me. About my intentions." He paced back and forth, then stopped to look at her. "You're looking for any reason to put distance between us again." His arms flew out to his sides before his hands landed on his hips.

Her mouth opened with the intent to refute him, but she knew he was right. It was second nature to raise her guards. She was embarrassed about losing her cool the night before, of needing his support. She was insecure about what his sister had said, how he'd responded. She was unsettled by whatever happened between him and the Sirkuhl, always feeling like an outsider.

Denial rose inside her, but she grabbed hold of it, and said instead, "I know." She looked down at the ground.

Her feelings were all mixed up. She used to be able to keep them in their proper places, but ever since they'd started working together, she was struggling. And worse, even if she wanted to win this thing, she wasn't sure she could keep her feelings contained any longer. She wasn't sure she wanted to. She was so tired. "You're right."

"I don't–" He clamped his mouth shut and huffed his frustration before turning away from her, crossing his arms over his chest, and dropping his head forward. She resisted the urge to go to him and lay her hands against his wide back, to comfort him as he had done for her, but the *why* behind his rejected countenance was evasive.

After a beat, she said, "I don't mean to do it, but trusting people is difficult."

He didn't move.

She moved instead so they were shoulder-to-shoulder, facing the thick vines of the milsk. She reached out and touched one of the wide, white blossoms. It closed at her touch. "I'm trying here. I'm just not very good at it." She leaned forward so she could see his eyes.

He glanced at her, solemnity riding his brow, making it heavier than usual.

She smiled, though it was small and slight. "Vempur, Jenna, and Tsua probably have a few stories about my neurosis."

He took another deep breath, then said, "That isn't surprising, Ima, with everything you've gone through.

I'm sorry for getting upset. I didn't mean it. It was–" He didn't finish the thought but turned to face her, dropping his arms– "I'm just sorry. I didn't mean to make you feel left out."

"Thanks for that. It doesn't matter." She had to look away from him, because she suddenly wanted to reach out and touch him again, recalling the feel of his body against hers when he'd held her. She studied her hands instead. "We won." She tilted her face up and grinned.

He stepped closer, and her breath pulled up short.

She fought against the urge to step closer, holding her ground instead.

"It matters," he said, his eyes moving over her features.

She could almost feel his look like a caress, and her breath moved through her like she'd just run a race into the high peaks of the Lopah. Her heart raced right along with her breath.

"It matters because you matter," he finished, his gaze dropping to her mouth before lifting back to her eyes.

Imogene's insides melted, poured from her shoulders, and pooled into her feet. She thought about all the feelings swirling through her. Feelings she'd had about Timaeus for a long time and stamped down into a hiding place she carried around inside of her, feelings she'd hidden in performance and anger. The hiding place had been revealed.

She could blame their victory, the heightened emotions about what had just happened, and maybe under different circumstances, she wouldn't have done it, but for once in her life, she didn't think. She just moved.

Grasping his face in her hands, she drew him closer. "Kiss me, Kade."

"It's Timaeus." His hands framed her face, and his gorgeous mouth finally met hers.

The kiss. Oh, the kiss was like a storm in the desert—a flash flood, lightning flashing, illuminating shadows and sizzling the world around them. She hadn't known, and if she had, she would have insisted on kissing Timaeus way before this.

And she would have continued kissing, reveling in the feel of his strong shoulders, the width of his neck, the way his smooth skin accommodated hers, offering the most addictive sensations. The way his hair was soft at his nape against her palms and made her want to run her hands over it repeatedly. The way his hands moved from her face, ran the length of her arms, and dropped to her hips, squeezing, pulling her closer, so there wasn't space between them.

But then he ended it, his forehead to hers. He took a deep breath and stalled there, just breathing, eyes closed, and didn't say anything.

A heartbeat later, he leaned back, his dark eyes moving across her face, stopping at her lips, his chest heaving as if he had just finished the same race she'd also run. She was sure he would kiss her again, wanted him to, but instead of closing the distance, he stepped away, ran both hands over his hair with a heavy sigh, and turned away.

"Stars," he swore, more on a breath than with the deep tone of conviction.

Confusion slapped her. She touched her lips with her fingertips.

"I'm sorry," he said. "This is just too complicated."

"What?"

His words weren't connecting with the pace of her mind, which was knee deep in the quicksand of the kiss. The residual electricity of the lightning strike still burned through her.

"I shouldn't have. I mean–" He sighed, running a hand over his face. "I'm not saying this right."

His response left her with an assumption: he hadn't been as affected by the kiss as she had been. Maybe hadn't wanted to kiss her. One-sided desire mortified her. She crossed her arms over her chest, stepped back, and turned away, facing the milsk blossoms, wishing for a moment she could go back in time to when they looked prettier. Her face was hot with embarrassment. "Oh. I see."

"No. No, Ima." He grasped her elbow and tried to turn her to face him.

She jerked out of his grip. "Don't."

Her eyes blurred with self-recrimination. She knew better. She'd always known better. She had no wish to add to her shame. Kade represented everything in her world that wouldn't work. He was from a powerful family. He had a name. Everything would come easy to him because of who he was. And everything in her life was like climbing uphill without reprieve. She'd known better than to nurture any feelings, and she'd done it anyway.

"Ima, please," Kade pleaded from behind her. "It isn't what you think."

"No?" She whirled on him. "And what is it?"

His mouth opened, then shut. Then opened again when he started, "I just—"

"It's complicated." She took a step back and shook her head. "I get it. Just a game like everything else around here. No worries, Kade." She looked down at the ground and continued her backward trek. "Doesn't mean anything. Too distracting. Whatever excuses come to mind." She looked up then, willing the threatening tears to remain behind her eyes. "We should just be friends anyway. Don't need to complicate things."

"That's not what I was going to say—"

"I am. Saying it." She turned so she wouldn't have to face him. Slagging feelings. She didn't need them. Knew it all along. She tried to swipe at the tears without him noticing as she walked away.

"Imogene, please," he called after her.

She didn't look back, just waved him off and kept walking.

20

REALITY

Imogene slammed the button to close the door, leaning her forehead against it as soon as it did. The surface was cool and refreshing, but it didn't keep the tears from filling her eyes and spilling down her cheeks. Her room felt more like a prison than a place of refuge after kissing Kade, which was on a loop in her mind. The kiss. The feelings. The rejection. She would rather be anywhere other than confined to her room, but she didn't have anywhere else to go. Vempur's room would have been her first choice, but he and Jenna were still running the trial. And Tsua wasn't the kind of friend to offer comfort.

A knock at the door made her jump.

"Ima. May I talk to you? Please."

Kade.

"I think we said more than enough," she retorted, trying to disguise the emotion in her voice with apathy, only it hitched on the last word, and she pressed a hand over her mouth.

"There's tons to say. I haven't even gotten started," he said from the other side of the door.

Needing to see him more than not, she swiped the tears from her face and opened the door.

He stood with his arms bracing each side of the door, his hair hanging slightly in his face. He looked much like he had when she'd left him, still in his competition clothes, only now he had an undone quality defining his usually crisp edges. But that unreadable expression that always plagued her was back on his face, intense and enigmatic.

It had always driven her crazy, wishing she'd had the key to unlock it, and now she realized, he'd given it to her somewhere between sparring and the kiss. He'd allowed her inside. That thought, and the way he was looking at her, had her stomach twisting itself into knots wanting to step closer rather than away from him like she knew she should.

"Five minutes." She stepped back to give him space to enter and looked down at the floor to keep from looking at his lips and recalling that kiss.

"That won't be enough time, but I'll take it." He pushed off the doorway and walked past her. "You didn't let me talk. You walked away." He turned, his hands framing his hips.

She crossed her arms over her chest and didn't respond.

"Nothing to say?" He mirrored her, crossing his arms.

"This is me giving you your five minutes," she snapped. "You've got so much to say apparently."

He took a frustrated breath, running his palms over his face, scraping the stubble before he pushed his hands to tug at his hair. It remained a mess. "Stars. You can be so infuriating."

Imogene waited for him to continue but was struck by his emotion as his mask fell away, allowing her inside once more. Kade was always the pinnacle of control. Always had been. It had been one of the reasons she was so jealous of him, his ability to appear so calm, cool, and collected no matter the circumstances.

Except for now.

He turned away from her, made a frustrated sound, then swung back. "I messed up, Ima."

She pressed her teeth together.

"But not how you think."

"And how do I think?"

"You made it clear earlier. You think I don't like you." He stepped closer. "That the kiss meant nothing."

She held her ground and narrowed her eyes.

"I like you, Ima. I like you so fucking much that kissing you was everything. I've wanted to kiss you since I saw you in year two rappelling from the Mountain against Dwellen. And you smoked him because he was scared of heights."

She relaxed and fought a smile, having forgotten that.

"Or when you were awarded the Year Three medal of honor because you helped your unit win the final trial that year. Or every time I saw you walking across the quad with your friends, or every time you stood up for Vempur when someone was razzing him." His voice was gentle, and his eyes measured her.

"You said you only noticed me after sparring a few weeks ago."

"I lied."

"What are you saying?" She released her arms to her sides. She wanted to take his face between her hands and kiss him again.

But she was afraid.

"That I like you. That I wanted to kiss you, and I want to kiss you again." He took another step toward her.

She held her ground, letting him closer, wanting him closer. But then her fear took over, his earlier words, his actions adding bricks to her walls. She stepped back.

He looked down, his chin dipping to his chest. "I want that so much, but it's also complicated."

"Because I'm Imogene Sol," she said with enough derision lacing her voice that he looked up, his features weighted with a deep frown.

"What's that supposed to mean?"

"You're a Kade. A Legacy. And I'm... not."

He took a step back. "No. No." He shook his head. "Is that what you think?"

"Take a walk in my shoes."

He scoffed. "You're so far off base." He smiled, but it held no joy or humor in it. "I can't tell you all of what I want."

"That's stupid, Kade."

"It's Timaeus, Ima, and no, it isn't, because if you were in my shoes, I know for a fact you'd understand." He stopped and looked up at the ceiling, then back at her. Then he sighed. "I'm on assignment. It isn't for the school. It's for something else, and I can't compromise it by telling anyone."

This hurt. Like so many of her classmates, he had an early placement—one that already had him at work—and she was still fighting for hers.

She took a step back, hitting the wall. "You're a Legacy placement." It proved once again how alone she was, reiterating why she'd always needed to do this on her own.

His eyebrows shifted over his eyes with concern and confusion. "Yes."

She turned away from him. He had nothing to lose, while she had everything. And she'd been willingly walking into losing it because of her feelings for him.

"That's what upsets you? My placement? Not that I like you or that I want to kiss you or that I'm trying to do the right thing because I don't want to lie to you?"

"Not your placement."

"Then what?"

"The fact that you have to ask says everything."

"Have you solved the puzzle box yet?" His eyes skittered around the room.

"What does that have to do with anything? It isn't like I've had a ton of time, but yours is almost up."

He pressed his teeth together, the skin of his jaw protruding.

"So you have been lying," she said, catching on that truth.

He turned, his hand in his hair again. "Yes, but–"

"There isn't a 'but'–"

He turned back to her. "Really? So final, Imogene. You aren't even willing to trust me. You never will... because I'm a Kade? You won't consider if you were in my shoes–"

"But I'm not!" she yelled, her hands flailing out to

her sides. "I never have been. I don't have two parents and three siblings. I'm no Legacy. My parents were traitors and are slagging dead. I'm just trying to make something of this life I've been given!"

"And I am just trying to help you."

"By lying?"

"In this case, yes."

"Do you hear yourself?"

"I'm pretty self-aware, Imogene. Are you?"

"What's that supposed to mean?"

But he didn't answer, just shook his head.

She cursed the tears that made another appearance, turning away from him and swiping at her eyes once more, fearing the weak feeling they gave her. She kept her back to him and said, "I think you should go."

"Ima." His tone was the one she loved. Patient and somehow vulnerable. "Talk to me, please. Really talk to me."

"How?" she asked, turning toward him. "When you can't do the same?"

He stepped up to her and framed her face with his hands, swiping at her tears with his thumbs, his eyes diving deeper into hers. "Please, Ima. Don't shut me out until you have all the facts."

She jerked her head out of his touch but couldn't keep the tears from falling and swiped at them with her fingers. "Please. Just go."

He was silent, then until he sighed and said, "Those

walls you've got up are going to keep good people out. Maybe you don't trust me, but if you don't start learning to let people in, Imogene, you're going to find yourself alone." His eyes pleaded with her a moment before shuttering closed once more. "Then again, maybe that's what you want."

Then he was gone.

She sank down onto her bed and cried.

She was alone. She had worked so hard. She had kept most at arm's length for a variety of reasons, but what he said was right: she was protecting herself from the hurt of losing him. Of losing herself. Like the loss of her parents and everything that loss represented. But she'd always been alone.

Somehow, when she was all cried out, she'd managed to shower and change. Then she grabbed the puzzle box, if at least to occupy her thoughts. She looked for her old code-breaking notes buried in the archives of her files, and after a few hours, found a few and reviewed different cipher systems, then looked up other systems, adding to her old notes. She tested out one style on the word, but it didn't work. Then another without success.

When her friends knocked at her door, she was blurry eyed with research and no closer to solving the puzzle. She put everything away and opened the door to Vempur and Jenna who filed through engaged in a conversation about the trial. They were smiling and laughing as usual. She felt outside of it, morose in her isolation and sadness about Kade, which she didn't want to admit to. She couldn't find it in her heart to care anymore, the apathy of feeling so removed.

"Where's Tsua?" she asked.

"Had to do something for his halo," Jenna said and sat down next to Vempur on the floor.

"We saw Kade a little while ago at the Globe. He looked like I usually look when I've had a run in with Dwellen. Not the look of someone who took first place in the Trial of Fortitude." Vempur said. "Congratulations, by the way. First! And not a single penalty. That must be a record."

Imogene harrumphed at him.

"It is." Jenna shared a look with Vempur. "You're looking like someone broke into the com-server and reassigned you to last place in the class," Jenna said. "What happened?"

"What?" Imogene asked. "Nothing."

"How's that going?" Vempur asked. "With Kade?"

"Nowhere."

Jenna sat up. "What? Why?"

"Have you guys forgotten? It's the Trials, and my ass is on the line? I mess up, and I'm going to Carnos as a plebe. Also, someone is trying to make sure that happens. Timaeus has his Legacy placement just because he's a Kade. You all have your placements. I'm the one with no prospects." She didn't want her voice to shake, but it did. "I can't let anything get in the way of that."

Her friends watched her with serious looks on their faces, their smiles having faded to nothing.

"Did you just call him Timaeus?" Vempur asked.

She narrowed her eyes and just for spite replied, "Not even *Kade*."

"Imogene," Jenna said quietly. "Your win today solidified your top ten placement for the final trial. What more do you need to prove? You'll get a placement."

Her eyes jumped between her friends. What was she still trying to prove? She may not be winning as number one, but she was in the top ten—most likely back in the top five with this last trial's performance. That was surely good enough to get a good placement. She'd done it. But despite everything she'd accomplished, she felt no closer to what she needed.

Jenna and Vempur were still watching her, but now their gazes were worried.

"I'm still waiting for an answer to the question." Vempur set his Com down in his lap and crossed his long legs in front of him.

"I don't know," Imogene answered. "It used to be really clear."

"What did it used to be?" Jenna matched Vempur's body language, so they were mirrors of one another.

Imogene reached up and plucked her sweater from the seat on her desk and slipped into it, needing the comfort of it around her as she resettled on the bed. "To succeed. To get a good placement. To make—" Her throat closed around the words: *my parents*. How did you make your dead parents proud? And your dead, traitor parents at that? She looked from Jenna's foot tapping against Vempur's, then at their faces. "I didn't want anyone to say I was a traitor. Like them."

"No one has called you that since we were Year Threes, Sol." Vempur was watching Jenna's foot tap his. "Is it because of how others treat you? Or what you think about yourself?"

Unsettled by his question, Imogene reared back.

"I realized something today," Vempur said.

"You did?" Jenna asked.

Imogene noticed a smile shining Jenna's eyes. "What happened on your trial?" she asked.

Vempur smiled, his black eyes sparkling at Jenna. "Yes, Jenna, I do learn, despite what you say."

"Are you two flirting?" Imogene asked, her eyes jumping between them and their silly grins.

Jenna shrugged and smiled at Vempur.

Vempur's umber skin turned darker. "Anyway..." He looked back at Imogene. "I've known for a long time that there's no going it alone. You taught me that, Sol. My first friend here, my sister. You've always had my back when I didn't have my own. And on this last trial, Jen had my back."

"Jen?" Imogene looked at Jenna's glowing face.

Vempur continued. "I realized when we crossed that finish line we're leaving soon. You won't always be around, or Jenna, or Tsua. I'm going to be on my own again."

"You're my family," Imogene said.

"Yes, but this moment here, it will be gone. Every moment we've already shared is filed away into the memory bank. We're moving on, starting new files somewhere else."

"You're not making me feel better," Imogene told him.

"I'm not trying to, Sol."

"Then what are you trying to do?"

"To tell you to change your script. You aren't fighting the same battle anymore, but you're acting like that's the only battle to fight. If you keep fighting it, you're going to lose everything that is important, and you will be alone." Vempur leaned forward. "And like you taught me, no one can go it alone. We need one another. We need the next tribe we build." His message was so much like Kade's.

"What are you saying?"

Vempur looked down at Jenna. "I'm tired of playing it safe," he said, then leaned over and pressed a kiss to Jenna's mouth.

"Oh. Wow." Imogene arched her eyebrows. "Got it. Flirting."

Vempur pulled away and studied Jenna's beaming

face.

"Please don't tell me that was your first kiss," Imogene said.

"Nope," Vempur admitted. "About the 100th."

"What?" Her eyes leaped to Jenna. "This is who you were waiting on?"

Jenna blushed, then nodded. "We didn't want to unnecessarily complicate the friend group with any drama should this not have worked."

"Because Imogene will always choose me," Vempur said.

Jenna gave him a playful swat but didn't argue the point.

Vempur took Jenna's hand, then looked at Imogene. "Life's too short."

"Are you saying I shouldn't have assumed that Kade is lying to me?"

"I think he's an ass," Vempur smiled, "but he's an honorable one. Maybe he deserves to be given the benefit of the doubt?" He paused, then said, "But this isn't about Kade, Imogene, it's about you. You don't have to fight the legacy of your parents just like I don't have to keep telling myself I'm unworthy of wanting more. We don't have to lug around those bags we were carrying at fifteen like shields anymore. I don't want to walk into the next phase of my life still carrying it. Do you?"

"When did you get to be so wise?" Imogene asked.

"I've always been this wise."

"It's really hot," Jenna said.

"Stop. Please," Imogene smiled. "Or take those oogley eyes out of my vicinity."

After they left holding hands, Imogene noted with a shudder, she lay in her bed thinking about Timaeus Kade, while fiddling with the puzzle box. She'd spent her entire cadet career competing with him. She supposed it was because she admired him, always had. His position, his name, the ease with which he navigated the world, and somewhere along the way it had morphed from admiration to jealousy. Her control, her struggle to let go, were all steeped in a past she was using like a weapon, and Vempur was right—it was a lie she was telling herself.

She'd earned her place before these Trials began. That hadn't been because of someone else. That hadn't been sabotaged. She'd performed, adapted, and survived, and whatever happened after the Trials were over would be what it would be, even if it meant Sirkuhl Glyn recommended her to Carnos. She'd be the best damned officer Carnos had ever seen.

She took a deep breath, ready to face her final trial, and give it her best, not because she had something to prove to anyone else, but because she needed to do it for herself.

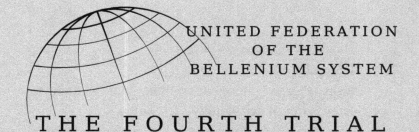

UNITED FEDERATION OF THE BELLENIUM SYSTEM

THE FOURTH TRIAL

The Final Trial at the Academy showcases the top ten cadets in the recruiting class—the best & brightest. A team trial, the remaining leaderboard students are split into two teams to complete an assignment in tandem. A panel of observers rank each cadet on criteria measuring teamwork, leadership, physical & mental ability, adaptability, communication, grace under pressure, & other qualities sought within the Federation. This task serves to determine final cadet-class rankings & distinctions. This is the final Year 7 assignment before promotion.

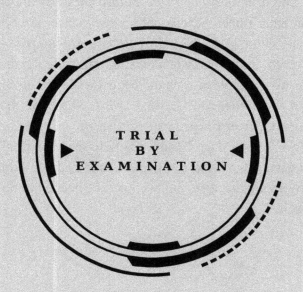

TRIAL BY EXAMINATION

21

THE FINAL TRIAL

The next few turns were a slide back into how things used to be, only Imogene couldn't slide back into losing her new understanding. Like watching Kade across the Globe with his unit, dressed in his gray fatigues, relaxed and confident as always. Her first impulse had been bitterness, but she checked herself. Though raw with new hurt, she wasn't angry at Kade for being honest with her, even if she hadn't liked what he'd said.

She didn't hate him. She hated that her feelings made her feel afraid and weak. She hated that she'd pushed him away and ruined what had bloomed between them. His words crashed around inside her: *I wanted to kiss you. I didn't want to lie.* He'd been a friend. She hadn't. And if there had ever been someone to trust, she'd done a great job of pushing him away. All because she'd been afraid.

Stupid, Sol.

His eyes slid to her, stopped, and lingered a moment before he turned back to his unit.

At that moment, she felt hopeful that maybe there was still a chance to fix this mistake. But she also knew she couldn't think about that just then. She had a final trial to face. So rather than fixate on watching him, on thinking about what to say, she busied herself. She walked the length of her cadet unit making sure everything was in order. "Straighten your shirt, Gronze," she told a year two. "Pemma, tie your boot laces before halo sees and makes you spit shine the whole unit," she warned a year three. After she'd walked the line, she stood at the back, at ease, and tried to keep her eyes from straying to Kade, except she couldn't seem to stop herself.

So she looked for Vempur.

He was across the room, standing at ease behind his unit. She couldn't really make out his features.

Then she looked for Jenna.

Then Tsua.

Each of them connected to the place in her heart that made her feel settled.

Her family.

Vempur was right. She'd lost sight of that.

She scanned the room, sitting in the moment.

When it came down to it, she'd met her goal. She was in the top five, sitting at four on the leaderboard. Maybe she didn't have her placement yet, but Jenna was right—she would earn one. Somewhere. Before the Academy, her life at the replacement facility had been bleak. Her prospects were worse: slated for the life of the bind, which really was no better than indentured servitude in the name of the Federation. But she'd made the cut after testing into the Academy, and a benefactor made sure she was able to get there.

When she'd first arrived, she was an angry girl with a lot to prove. The Academy as a means to an end. Seven years later, she was seeing it more clearly. What was next wasn't more of the same. It couldn't be. She was different.

"Attention," a halo called out.

The entire room shifted as one body, and it was something Imogene never tired of hearing. She loved it here. She loved her unit, helping the Year Ones when they were homesick, teaching the Year Fours to dig deeper when things got tough. It was satisfying. But she hadn't really given herself permission until this morning to consider what she would miss. She'd been so focused on doing well, on proving to everyone she could, on trying to prove she was more than what others thought that she'd missed out on a lot of the beauty of it. She'd missed out on what was truly important: what she thought of herself, which she understood to be a work in progress. How could she know when she'd spent so much time defining who she was against someone else?

"Cadets," Sirkuhl stated as he stopped on the dais at the front of the room. He led them through the Cadet recitation and the honor oath. "At ease," he said, and the room shifted again.

Two strangers—no, not strangers—stood near the entrance to the Globe. Mutez and Tynos. The Fourth Order officers watched, and when one of their eyes connected with hers, she snapped her gaze away, her heart picking up speed. She knew she wasn't guilty of anything, but their presence felt like a countdown of sorts. Had they found definitive evidence?

She waited for them to approach, but they didn't. They seemed to be waiting for something. Perhaps the end of the Sirkuhl's speech.

Her heartbeat echoed in her ears, making it difficult to concentrate.

"Today is the final trial for our Year Sevens." He paused. "Every year, this moment sits on my shoulders with a weight of poignancy. I've had the honor of watching each cadet grow and develop into the strong

Year Sevens who will move out into the system to serve the Federation. And this year's group is no different, though perhaps it hits a little closer to home than usual."

Imogene glanced at the other Year Sevens around her. Everyone shrugged, not sure what had gotten into their commanding officer. He always shared his final trial speech, but this one seemed a bit more emotional, and Glyn wasn't known for emotion if it wasn't irritation, annoyance, frustration, or good old solid anger.

He cleared his throat of whatever was weighing his emotions and moved back into his usual speech. "Year Ones, you're close to transition to Year Two and will be who next year's Year Ones look to emulate. Each of you is moving toward that Year Seven threshold. The trial today will offer a lesson for all of us as our leaders participate in a realistic simulation design to test their mettle and showcase the reason they are on the leaderboard. Our best and brightest. Be sure to make it to the screening room on time. The feeds will disseminate it live. Halos, please prepare your cadets, and Year Sevens not in the sim, please be on hand. With that, let's eat. Good luck and endure."

The Academy of cadets repeated the last phrase.

"Dismissed."

The room erupted with sound as each cadet found their friends and tables to await their turn to get their meal.

Struggling to concentrate with so much at stake, Imogene considered seeking out Timaeus to talk, but she decided it wasn't time. She needed to focus on herself, on her own performance for this competition, and with the Fourth Order presence, she was going to struggle. Deciding she'd find him after the trial was completed, she escaped the cafeteria to find space in her own room to go through her breathing exercises and visualization techniques to center herself.

The Fourth Order didn't follow.

She wasn't sure if she was relieved.

At the appointed time, she reported to the sim room. Inside were several spaces mocked up into the bridge of a Federation ship. For the trial there were two bridges, both Devastator class IX command centers.

Dressed in gray fatigues like the rest of the leaders lining up with her, she stood at ease at one end of the line. Aware of Timaeus the moment he entered, she felt the warmth of his gaze when he looked at her. When he found a space to wait at the opposite end of the line, she ignored the disappointment, recalling the third Trial when he'd come to find her.

She didn't allow herself to wallow there, however. She was a Ring Academy Year-Seven Cadet. So was he. They both had a job to do, which meant personal feelings needed to be put aside. Now, she had to focus on the trial.

"Welcome to the final task." Halo Tand's voice

grabbed their attention and waited for all of them to gather around them. "You have been split into two units and assigned roles by the commander, which I will share with you momentarily. It is important to note that both units are working toward the same goal as compatriot ships working in concert for a common purpose. This isn't a competition against each other, but rather a showcase of your leadership and abilities within the confines of a team. Your actions, behaviors, decisions, and words will impact your final scores. Assessors will be watching from the feeds as well as the perimeter of the simulation, keeping score. Understood?" Halo Tand waited a moment before continuing.

Several Fourth Order officers entered the room, catching Imogene's attention. She tensed and looked straight ahead at the sim, willing herself to focus, but her thoughts were spinning with questions. Her gaze drifted to Timaeus, who was staring at her. He shook his head and mouthed: *focus*. She offered a slight nod, grateful for his friendship even amid conflict. Hopeful that if the Fourth Order were here to arrest her, she would get to tell him that.

"In today's simulation, a secret missive gathered by Federation intelligence describes the location where captured Federation officials are being held by a terrorist group. The mission will deploy two Devastator class IX ships on a rescue mission, one for retrieval of the Federation officials and the other for cover."

Imogene's eyes slid to a Fourth Order officer near the door, then she shook her head. *Focus!*

"The object of your sim today is to cooperate to complete the mission. Each Devastator Crew is to assume they have troops and operatives at the ready for whatever obstacles the sim executes.

Imogene's Com beeped, followed by a succession of beeps from each of the cadets.

"Your Com has queued up your mission card and objective, your group, your rank, and position. The rules stipulate that your assigned rank will hold as true for the duration of the simulation, and the contents of the message on your Com, aside from your rank and position, are to remain confidential. Questions?"

Imogene waited to be directed to check her Com. A cold sweat broke out on her brow as her gaze jumped to the Fourth Order officers leaning against the outer wall. There were four of them spaced out.

Focus, Imogene.

She had to keep herself together.

"Halo Butresh is uploading your protocol briefs. Please open your Com and report to duty," Tand directed and stepped off the simulation stage.

Imogene opened the file on her Com and read:

Commander Imogene Sol, *First Commander of the Orion XI, Devastator class 9 ship in the Federation Fleet.*

Officers in order of rank:
First Officer: Dwellen Ridig
Security and Intelligence Officer: Timaeus Kade
Communications & Technology Officer: Bennisha Poli
Pilot: Ravi Doxen

Working in concert with *Commander* Hemsen Dennison *and crew of the Eos IV, Devastator class 9 ship in the Federation Fleet.*

Notes: You are a brand-new commander, and this is your first mission; all your officers know this. Your first commander was not your selected first but has served the Orion XI with distinction for the last four flight cycles. Apart from the communications officer, you have only just met the other officers.

Good luck on your mission. Endure.

Imogene slipped her nameplate—Commander Sol—into the space above the pocket of her shirt and glanced around, her nerves nipping at all the spaces under her skin they could find. Halo Butresh uploaded her brief—notes for their role and possible scenarios for support. Timaeus met her gaze. She took a deep breath, and with her Com in hand made her way to the appropriate stage.

Focus, Imogene, she coaxed herself once more, but heard a combination of voices in her head: *You've trained for this. You deserve to be here no matter what happens after.*

She took her place with the other cadets in the ship simulator. A countdown appeared on the ship viewport from ten to zero.

The Trial by Examination had begun.

22

TRUST

Forgetting she was in the midst of a Trial was too easy. The sim room was dimmed but for the lights on the ship where Imogene sat with her teammates, strapped into seats as light blurred in the viewer surrounding them, as if they were hurtling through Federation space, she had to remind herself it wasn't real. Though each of them held a Com—which held their protocol handbook—it was the only thing to remind them they were in a simulation.

"Commander," Dwellen said, sitting to her right on the bridge of the ship. "We're coming out of hyper."

Imogene glanced at Dwellen, who wasn't her enemy here. He looked at her expectantly—the usual hostility and bitterness missing from his features. Instead, he waited for her—as much as everyone else in the sim— as if she were truly their commander. Here, they were teammates, and he was holding to his role, doing the job he'd been assigned. While it was difficult to separate what had come between them before, she knew it was a necessity in order to do the job.

She glanced at her Com for the prompt. "Time? Remaining distance?" she asked, then glanced out the viewport programmed to show the slowing of the ship as they entered the identified system, a planet coming into view.

She glanced at Dwellen again, who looked at the computer at his station. He typed in information, and she noticed the slight tremble of his hand as he did. The realization that Dwellen Ridig was as nervous as she was hit her hard. The entirety of her time at the Academy, she'd felt as if she didn't belong, as if she was somehow inferior and needed to prove herself. In her mind, the other cadets did belong. They knew their place and were secure in their status, but seeing Dwellen— blustery, fiery, jerk that he'd been—trembling told her a new story. One she'd never even considered. Everyone was as scared as she was.

She swallowed.

Dwellen glanced between the ship computer at his station to his Com aligning the information the computer offered with the protocols in the Com. When he finally looked up, he said, "We'll have an estimated 120 snaps to planet intercept."

She unstrapped herself along with the rest of her crew and turned to face Kade, her Security and Intelligence Officer. Taking another deep breath, she consulted her protocol. "Any word on the surface team?"

When she looked up from her reader to Kade, he offered her a small smile, one that felt like a secret, one that felt like before their fight. He glanced down at his Com. "Not since hyper and Com silence is in effect until"–he paused consulting the computer– "60 snaps to intercept."

"Prepare your ship team," she told him.

With a nod, he turned and began typing into the computer, which she knew was recording everything.

Her heart bounced around in her chest with that nervous energy, which was gaining momentum, crashing against her ribs. They were being watched, judged. She'd spent her life being judged as a Sol, and the thought made her chest tighten with panic. What if she failed? What if she ruined this for everyone else?

She squeezed her hands into fists, wishing she were in the sparring room instead. That would be easier than this. That was only about her and her opponent. If she failed, she had only herself to blame, only her place on the leaderboard impacted, but she wasn't there. Her performance could impact the entire team. Her mind reeled as she shut her eyes.

"Commander?"

Imogene opened her eyes, which collided with Kade's. He smirked at her and raised an eyebrow with a cocky tilt to his head. His look was exactly what she needed to remind her who she was… a fighter, even here.

You can do this.

With a deep breath, she relaxed her hands and turned to another teammate. "Officer Poli."

"Commander?" Bennisha replied, turning from her control panels on the bridge.

"Is the Eos in range?"

"Yes, Commander."

"Hail them on the Com."

"Right away." Bennisha turned to her notes and pressed her buttons.

Hemsen's face appeared on the viewport. "Sol," he said, and Imogene had the impression he'd been a commander for years. "You hailed, Orion?"

She suppressed a smile. "Orion offers gratitude for your assistance today."

He smiled back. "Orders are orders, and the Eos has been ordered to take cover on this mission. Our SIO is ready to run support."

The viewport went dark.

"Where is he? Status report Com?" she called out.

"We've lost power," Bennisha replied.

"Systems roll call," Imogene ordered. "Any other power outages?"

Each system checked in with their functionality—the issue targeted at Communication.

She looked at her notes. "Ridig?" she asked and glanced from her notes to Dwellen. "Com insight?"

He looked up from his reader, his blue face pale, his eyes wide with panic. He'd lost his place. "I don't–"

Imogene stalled, her eyes on Dwellen. Every terrible thing he'd done to her flashed through her mind. The workout all those weeks ago. Seven years of his bullying of her and Vempur. With all that history, she could let him fail, let him flounder through. Her heart picked up speed at the prospect of getting even with him, but suddenly Vempur's words came back to her: *You aren't fighting the same battle anymore, but you're acting like that's the only battle to fight. If you keep fighting it, you're going to lose everything that is important, and you will be alone. No one can go it alone. We need one another.*

Just like sitting on the plains with Kade getting shot at hadn't only affected her, this Trial, all of them were tied to each other. They were all cadets at the Academy. They were all Year Sevens. They were all going to be a part of the Federation in some capacity. They were all afraid and unsure, including Dwellen. Perhaps he didn't deserve mercy. Who truly did? But they all certainly needed it.

And she couldn't lose sight of that. Not now.

"Ridig!" she snapped, to stop what appeared to be a spiral and took a step closer to his station, then another, probably the closest to Dwellen she'd ever chosen to be in all their years at the Academy. "Look at me. Focus on me," she told him quietly.

Dwellen's dark eyes jerked from the Com to her.

"You're my first officer. You know this ship inside and out, including any bugs. I need you and your expertise now."

He nodded, drawing in a deep breath, and looked down at the computer, then back at his Com. When he looked at her again, the panic had abated, his confidence returning. "The mainframe was updated during her last docking. Perhaps there's a bug."

Imogene nodded, looking at her protocol notes. "Get tech on it. We can't be dark for this mission. Poli, talk to me…"

When Hemsen's face finally came back into focus on the viewer, Imogene surveyed her team with pride before turning her attention to Hemsen, "Good to see you again, Orion."

"Commander," Kade said from his station. "SI reporting for duty."

"Is your team awake?" she asked.

"Roused and ready, Commander."

"Please confirm with the Eos SIO final prep for the upcoming tactical procedure. Then connect with the ground team."

Time passed, Imogene's pulse racing with each tactical decision she had to make. While her protocol handbook offered her insight in conjunction with the computer's simulation, ultimately those decisions came down to her choices. Sometimes she made them in concert with Hemsen, sometimes with Dwellen, but regardless the computer recorded it. And she wasn't alone. Each member of her team, their choices, their performance was being measured.

Kade scowled. The muscle in Dwellen's jaw ticked with tension. Poli tugged at her braids with each new challenge. Ravi's shoulders moved up and down, then she'd roll them to ease the tension. Despite every different obstacle, her team rallied and successfully navigated every challenge, every order Imogene gave them.

One hour. Two. The security and intelligence force deployed, leaving the simulation for another, connected to Imogene's ship only through their Coms just as they'd be in a real mission.

"We've got company," Ravi called out. "Two ships."

Imogene crossed the bridge to Ravi's piloting station to check the computer. "Hail the Eos."

"We see them," Hemsen's voice said over the intercom.

Imogene returned to her station and pressed the button to communicate with her security team. "Status?"

There was only static.

"Poli?"

"I'm on it," she said, her hands flying over her station to correct the issue.

"Kade? Come in."

Static.

"Poli?" Imogene repeated.

"Check now," Bennisha said, glancing over her shoulder.

"Status?"

Static.

But then it crackled. "Copy. Assets in hand," was Kade's reply.

"Get back to the ship."

The ship rocked as if fired upon, and Imogene grabbed the console to keep herself upright. "Slag. We're taking fire. Evasive action, Doxen."

"Copy," Ravi replied.

"Get your teams back to the ships. Now," she yelled

to Kade through the connection.

"Copy."

"Poli. Hail the transport team! Have them ready."

"Copy, Commander."

"Ridig, prepare the ship for battle. Doxen evasive maneuvering."

Another hit rocked the ship.

"Shields?" she asked.

"Holding," Dwellen replied.

In tandem, she and Hemsen led their ships through the fray of battle, her notes indicating her aim was to minimize ship damage and casualties. When another hit rocked the ship, Imogene glanced at her notes, suggesting the maneuver indicated in her script.

"Commander," Dwellen warned. "The ship isn't equipped for that kind of operation."

Encountering a moment when her knowledge of the ship was lacking and her notes were vague, she recalled Vempur's words: *you have to trust*. She recalled her notes: her first mission, her first officer familiar with the ship and its capabilities. She had to trust Dwellen and his judgment. "Make the call, Ridig."

Dwellen stepped up without hesitation. When he led them through successfully, Imogene heaved a sigh of relief.

"Get our teams," she ordered.

It was a dance between protocol handbooks, the simulation, and trusting her teammates, a give and take between expertise, roles, and assignments. When the mainframe failed, she looked to Poli to bring it back online. Enemy fire threatened; she relied on Dwellen's knowledge of their shields and weaponry to avoid becoming a sitting duck.

When both she and Hemsen led their ships to rendezvous, retrieved their security teams, and secured the Federation Officials, some of the tension left Imogene's shoulders. But it was only when Kade returned to the bridge that she could take a deep breath.

"The final Trial has concluded." The computer's detached tone echoed over the intercom as the regular lights brightened the sim room, revealing the stage and the room beyond, packed with people—including, Imogene noted with a sinking stomach, Fourth Order officers.

Slag.

23

DUPLICITY

Imogene stepped from the simulator and took a deep and contented breath. She'd laid it all on the line, and her score would be left up to the judges. She glanced around for the Fourth Order officers, content to face whatever she had to, but the officers didn't converge. Relieved but wary, she walked out into the hallway to find her friends waiting.

"Oh stars!" Jenna exclaimed. "That was incredible. I can't wait for you to watch that back."

"I don't think I can." Imogene smiled at her friend

and watched for Timaeus to emerge from the sim room.

She needed to talk to him.

"You must! I don't think I've ever been so proud." Jenna wrapped her arms around Imogene. "You looked like a commander. Maybe you'll receive a commission and that's why your placement has taken so long."

"As much as I love that idea, Jenna, I don't think I'd ever achieve clearance with my family history."

Dwellen emerged from the room and stopped.

She had this awful feeling that perhaps he was going to slip back into their former roles, but he surprised her by holding out his hand. "Good job, Sol."

She took it. "You too."

"Thanks for–"

"No thanks necessary," she interrupted. "You'd have done the same," she said, even though she wasn't sure that was the truth.

He offered a nod, a short but respectful smile, and walked away.

Vempur wrapped a strong arm around her. "He's still a slag, but that was classy, Sol. I'm so proud of you."

She looked up at Vempur and grinned, so grateful for him. For Jenna. For Tsua, who was looking at her with a frown. "Tsua? What's wrong?"

"Everything," he spat, his skin swirling black.

But she couldn't ask him to clarify because Sirkuhl Glyn arrived, and Tsua closed his mouth. "Sol."

They all saluted. "Sir."

"At ease. A good showing, cadet."

Unable to keep the smile from her face, Imogene replied, "Thank you, sir." But her eyes jumped to Tsua, who she could see was livid.

"You have made me excessively proud." The Sirkuhl offered her a smile and reached out to Tsua, placing a hand on his hoverboard as her friend swing the craft around, intending to leave. "Cadet Egroe. We have some things to discuss."

Imogene tensed as several Fourth Order officers converged, Mutez and Tynos among them.

She looked at the Sirkuhl. "I didn't do it, sir."

"I know, Sol," he said. "We know who did."

"Cadet Egroe," Officer Mutez said to Tsua, "we need you to come with us. We have some questions we'd like you to answer."

Imogene's mouth dropped open, and her gaze darted to Tsua whose skin was swirling with black and ribbons of red.

"What?" she choked out.

"What is going on?" Vempur asked, pushing off the wall.

No one responded.

"Tsua?" Jenna asked.

Tsua looked at Jenna and only Jenna. "It wasn't supposed to happen this way. She wasn't supposed to make it this far."

"What?" Jenna asked.

Imogene shivered, shocked, at the same time a warm presence moved in behind her. She knew it was Timaeus before she even turned to look. "What does that mean?"

Tsua looked at her. "Your villainous parents killed my mother," he spat, his skin flaring white.

"Wait. What?" Imogene took a step back, bumping into Timaeus behind her. "You said your mother died during the Dark War. Not Station 452."

"It's best if you don't say anything more, Egroe," Sirkuhl Glyn said. He looked at the Fourth Order Officers. "Please escort him to my office."

With Tsua's hoverboard secure, the Fourth Order escorted him down the hall.

Imogene shook her head. "Sirkuhl?"

Glyn looked at Kade then at her. "Come see me after the evening meal," he said. "We'll talk." Then he walked away.

Imogene covered her mouth, unsure what just happened. She stumbled backward into Timaeus, who grabbed hold of her, his arms around her from behind.

"I've got you," he said quietly.

"What the slag just happened?" Vempur asked.

Jenna wrapped her arms around his middle and buried her face in his chest. "Something bad. Something so bad."

"I don't know," Imogene said.

"I trusted him," Jenna said.

Imogene's eyes jumped to Jenna. Trust. Yes. "Me too."

"We all did," Vempur said, his words thick and marbly in his mouth, more growl than not. "I can't stay here. I feel like punching something." He turned and stalked down the hall toward the door. Jenna darted after him.

"Come on," Timaeus said. "I'll walk you to your room. We should get there before they let out the cadets. You're about to get swarmed."

She followed him in a daze.

When they reached her door, she flashed her Com, and the door slid open, then shut behind them. The lights flicked on. Imogene sat on the edge of the bed.

"What can I get you, Imogene?"

She shook her head. "I trusted him. I had no idea."

"No one did."

"But why would he…" Her eyes rose to meet his.

"I'm sorry, Ima."

She shook her head again. "I wanted to say I'm sorry to you. It all feels twisted now."

"Me?"

She looked down at her hands. "You were right, and I wanted to tell you I was sorry for being a bad friend…" She stopped, her mind spinning on all the times she was with Tsua, all the interactions, the ways they'd laughed together, playing Kobosham. "He let me win," she said.

Timaeus sat next to her on the bed and wrapped an

arm around her shoulders, pulling her into his side.

He didn't say anything even when it might have been tempting to fill the uncomfortable silence with placating words. But he comforted her with his presence instead, and Imogene was so grateful.

She cried. Timaeus held her. She slept. She dreamed.

In the dream...

Tsua was sitting on his hoverboard in the Codex, a Kobosham board between them. His skin was swirling with blue and green, the colors that told her he was happy. "You should count," he'd said, moving his pieces. "One. Two. Three."

"Why?" she'd asked and picked up the discarded pieces.

"Because you can hide in the numbers. That's what I would do."

The Codex shifted to computer code, vertical lines of symbols pulsing as it changed and rewrote, calculating, changing behind him.

"Why did you?" she'd asked him.

He turned black, but it wasn't like the swirl of his skin. He just turned black, blending in the background being overwritten by computer code. "There's a big hole in my heart," he'd answered. "Maybe if I solved the puzzle."

And suddenly he was gone, and panic slammed into her chest. "Tsua?"

She woke with a start, sitting up in her bed. Timaeus was gone.

She took several breaths to reorient to reality, the dream heavy in her mind. The puzzle box caught her gaze, along with a small pouch near it.

She stood and picked up the soft, green pouch. The contents shifted inside. Undoing the tie at the top, she drew it open, then dumped the contents into her palm. A bit of parchment and several marbles dropped into her hand. The note said:

> *I found some tiny planets for you, Imogene.*
> *Love, Timaeus*

Running her thumb along his script, she couldn't help but smile, even if it felt weighted with the gravity of painful emotion.

Then she looked at the puzzle box and recalled her dream. Numbers. And suddenly she knew how to solve the puzzle.

Pulling up a blank document on her Com, she wrote a simple code using the letters of the universal language with a corresponding number, then cross-referenced the ancient Lavi symbols for the numbers. Using the cipher—SURRECTION—she pressed the corresponding symbols in the correct order on the box.

It opened.

Inside was a coded message.

Imogene wrote the code out:

Welcome to Legion, Legacy.
Seek truth.

CLASSIFIED

L E G I O N

For 300 years, the UFB system worked, but as resources were used without thought to sustainability, the financial system was tapped. The Federation instituted Order 98.53B, which required all citizens to serve an additional four years in WorkForce Blind & Service Bind in order to tap into resources beyond the galaxy. Due to financial & food insecurity, as well as new raids by Outer Rim systems retaliating, civil unrest ignited in the Billenium System.

The rebellion took organized form in Legion & became a powerful terrorist organization gaining favor among the populace of the five systems, but was eventually thwarted by the Federation.

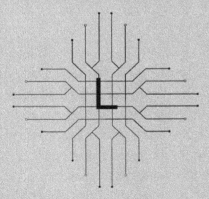

24

THE TRUTH

The door to Sirkuhl Glyn's office looked the same, a tall, dark, imposing barrier between the commander and everyone else. Imogene had been there a dozen times. She'd usually done something to deserve his admonishment, but this time she knew she wasn't there for that. This time the reason was because she needed clarity, and he'd invited her to seek him for it.

She needed to know what had happened with Tsua.

Sirkuhl Glyn's threat of Carnos still weighed on her, and she hadn't finished top in the Trials. The final leaderboard results had been posted during last meal. Her final placement was fourth behind Timaeus, Hemsen, and Ravi. Dwellen had also finished in the top five. She was content with her standing, but did it mean she was going to serve as a plebe on Carnos anyway? She was a Sol after all.

She straightened, smoothing her gray shirt, and took a deep breath. It didn't matter. Not really. She'd done her best, and she would continue to do her best moving forward no matter where she was.

Without any further hesitation, she knocked.

"Enter."

Imogene walked into his office and offered a salute. "Sir."

"At ease, cadet. Close the door and sit, please."

She did as he requested and sat in a chair, which was new. She didn't think she'd ever sat in his office.

"I'd rather not waste time on getting to the point, Sol. How are you doing? I know Egroe was your friend. It can be shocking when faced with such duplicity at the hands of someone you trusted."

"It was him?" Imogene adjusted in her seat and sucked in a deep breath. "All of it?"

The Sirkuhl sat back, relaxing, which was strange. "Most of it. He's confessed to messing with your pack for that first trial, hoping that alone would eliminate you. When it didn't, he hacked the file sent in your name."

"He sent the forged threat," she clarified.

The commanding officer nodded. "Confessed. Figured he had to do something more extreme to impact your place. And when that didn't keep you from competing, he manipulated the office break in."

Imogene's face reddened. "You knew?"

"Suspected. You don't get to where I am by being ignorant about what's happening around you, Sol."

"No, sir. I didn't–"

He held up a hand. "Egroe confessed he'd been trying to get you caught. He sent a message to my Com, thinking it would provide the evidence needed to get you kicked out. How did you get out of that one?"

Imogene would never reveal Timaeus's involvement. "Lucky, I guess."

The Sirkuhl made a noise that informed her he didn't believe her.

"Did he mess with the second and third Trials—the competitions?"

"No. That was me."

"What?"

"We… I suspected Egroe by then. Our team was busy working on decoding the hack, and we'd determined the motive."

"Which was the bombing?"

The Sirkuhl nodded. "His mother perished on

Station 452."

Imogene could have said 'So did mine,' but it failed to acknowledge Tsua's pain, his reason. "So, he blamed my parents, and by extension me."

"Grief and vengeance are rarely rational. So yes, he saw you as the embodiment of his loss. For a Mnemone like Egroe, taking your future from you would have squared away the debt owed for the loss of his family matriarch. By accomplishing this, he would have brought honor to his family."

"But why now? Why not a year ago? Three?"

"Maximum impact."

She swallowed, suppressing the tears, wondering how she hadn't seen it, but then neither had Vempur or Jenna. "And now?"

"His family won't shun him if that is what you're asking. They will understand his motivation."

"What will happen to him?"

"He is facing a Federation Tribunal."

"If he wanted me to fail, then why didn't he beat me at Kobosham?"

"Perhaps, Sol, you won that fair and square."

"But Tsua…"

"You believe he threw it?" When she nodded, he continued, "By allowing you to believe he'd thrown it, he offered you the reality that he was on your side."

"But what if I'd lost?" she asked.

"It was my hope you wouldn't, but I wasn't

worried."

Kade.

"So Tsua didn't throw it?"

"We tampered with the competition, placing you as his competitor. I wanted to see how he would respond either way."

"So did he throw it?"

"Does it matter if he did?"

Imogene swallowed. "I don't deserve to be in the top five if he did."

"As far as anyone is concerned, Sol, you won the competition. Egroe didn't. Whether he threw it is irrelevant and there's no way to prove it one way or the other."

"Why did you partner me with Kade?" she asked. "I was supposed to be with Dwellen."

"I was aware that things between you and Dwellen were tenuous, the workout a flash point."

"What? How?" But she knew. *Kade.*

He ignored her questions and continued. "I couldn't, in good conscience, pair you with a cadet that might impact your safety. Not with everything else."

She took a deep breath. "And the gun?"

"Strangely enough, completely random. A Federation peacekeeping unit was in the vicinity on their way into the valley," Sirkuhl Glyn explained. "They were running drills with the tech for an upcoming op and didn't know about the Trial or the possibility of cadets in the area."

Imogene could buy it. "What now?" she asked.

"For you? Whatever you want. You're top five in your class, Sol."

"But–"

"But?"

"I haven't gotten any offers, except for the Fourth Order."

"Which is back on the table," he said, "I mean, if you want it. They've offered a full apology." He punched some buttons on his desk Com, and a stack of files rose, hovering as holograms between them. There were several of them. "I've been holding onto them for you."

"But why?" Her eyes flew from the hologram to his face.

"I wanted the opportunity to speak with you first. To clear up some issues."

"But the Fourth Order–"

"I knew you were getting antsy."

"You threatened me."

He looked taken aback. "Threatened you?"

"With Carnos. After the workout."

He looked even more confused, which was out of character for him. "You thought me mentioning Carnos was a threat?" Glyn clarified.

"Yes, sir." Imogene felt the stirrings of more emotion. Anger, mostly, but confusion and anxiety.

"That was a pep talk."

"With all due respect, sir, that wasn't a pep talk."

He hummed a sound. "Maybe I need to work on my motivational support. I would never have threatened you, Imogene. You're–" He paused, that emotion clicking in the back of his throat, without any anger. "You're too important to me."

"I'm so confused, sir."

Glyn sighed, stood, and walked around his desk. He sat in the chair turned to face her, crossed his legs, and placed his hands in his lap. Then he just looked at her. "You really thought my Carnos speech was a threat?"

She looked up at him. "Yes, sir. I did."

He made another humming noise. "I knew your parents, Sol." His completely black eyes watched her. "Did you get the gift?"

The puzzle box.

She nodded. "You gave it to me?"

He didn't answer her question. "Did you open it?"

She nodded.

Glyn smiled, reached out, and placed something on the desk—a small, thin piece of tech no bigger than a fingertip. The desk Com went dark, but not just the hologram. Everything. The room stopped buzzing with tech, the lights going out so that all that remained was whatever light the windows offered. Turnus's rings glowed, and the light from the courtyard filtered into the room.

"What I'm about to tell you," Glyn started, "is classified. And truthfully, Imogene, this is out of order, but I believe you deserve the truth."

"Out of order?"

"You solved the puzzle?"

"What's Legion, sir?"

His grinned broadened. "Is that what the message said?"

She had so many questions but tried to keep them contained. "It said, 'Welcome to Legion, Legacy. Seek truth.'"

He grinned, a gentle one, and chuckled as he shook his head. "Of course it did."

"Excuse me, sir?"

"Let me preface this by saying, what I'm about to tell you is dangerous. It's out of order, because you shouldn't have access to it without proper protocols in place, but my gut tells me this is right. Do you want the information, Sol?"

Imogene swallowed, suddenly nervous. "Yes."

"Your parents worked for a deep cover operation."

"Is that what Legion is?"

"They were doing important work, Imogene. But they weren't traitors," he said not confirming or denying, but skipping over her question. "They were officially killed in the line of duty trying to stop the 452 bombing—which wasn't set by the Legion, only made to look that way—that's what it says in their true file."

"Wait. What?"

Sirkuhl nodded. "Not everything is as it seems."

"You knew them?" she asked.

He nodded. "Some of my dearest friends."

Puzzle pieces began to take shape in Imogene's mind, sliding into place. "You're my benefactor?"

"One of them."

"One?"

"Your parents acquired many friends over their lifetime."

"Why keep that a secret?"

Glyn didn't answer.

"You can't say?"

He smiled. "I can't tell you everything you want to know unless you accept the call."

"Legion? My parents were Legion?"

"You're catching on."

"I'm a Legacy?"

He grinned. "I attended this very institution with your parents."

"They went here?"

He nodded. "Yes, and like you, flirted with their standings on that leaderboard. Some of the best." Glyn smiled at whatever he was remembering, then it faded. "They've been scrubbed."

"Erased from the archives."

"Mostly."

"By Legion?"

"I can't answer that."

"The Federation." Imogene sat on that nugget, then asked, "Why did the message say, 'Seek truth'? Is that what it means?"

"We'll leave that for later," he said, lifted a finger to silence her, then removed the scrambler. The desk Com, the lights, the hum of the tech jumped back to life. "So as you can see, you have some decisions to make. I'm proud of you, Imogene. Your accomplishments here are paramount. Your placement on the leaderboard, your resilience in the field despite the hardships you faced, and your demonstration in the simulation today. I've been fielding recruitment calls all year, and you will have a choice of what you would like to do."

Tears filled her eyes, but she didn't want to allow them space. Not in front of her commanding officer—found-uncle—whatever he was. Shock, relief, disbelief all swirled like a whirlpool inside her with the sadness and horror of what she'd learned and been through, none of them landing. Instead, everything was drawing her into the chaotic center. "I don't know what to think."

Sirkuhl Glyn stood and returned behind his desk where he tapped on the desk screen. "Well, you can begin by reading through the documents I've just dropped into your Com."

Her Com beeped.

"That will keep your brain busy until the final transition ceremony. You've got at least four official offers there with enough reading for another year at the Academy. And after you've gone through that, you'll need to decide what you want."

She leaned back in the chair, unsure where to begin, her thoughts a tumultuous tumble inside her head, making her brain hurt. She had choices. It was all so much.

"I can see you're trying to process what you've learned. I suggest some time to formulate your questions. I'm not going anywhere, so come find me if you want to talk through things."

"Yes, sir."

"You are free to leave, Sol."

She stood.

"And Imogene—"

She stopped and looked at him.

"—one of those placement options is a halo position here at the Academy. Maybe consider it? We'd be honored to have you."

She nodded. "Thank you, sir."

He returned his attention to his desk, and she left, closing the door before turning around.

Across the hall, leaning against the wall with his hands in his pockets and his booted feet crossed at the ankles waited none other than Timaeus Kade.

25

WHAT MATTERS

Imogene stopped short, ecstatic to see him, but also aware there were so many things still to say. There was the residual fear lingering and hurting having been duped by Tsua, telling her to keep guarding the new raw and vulnerable parts of herself.

But Timaeus had been there that very afternoon, helping her stand, and he was here now, even after she'd pushed him away with her fear.

"How are you?" he asked, clearly waiting and slightly hesitant. Worried.

"I'm not sure. Why?"

"I'm afraid Egroe ruined all my good work. And I'm hoping that isn't the case."

"What do you mean?"

"Ima."

"What are you doing?" she asked.

"Isn't it obvious?" He pushed away from the wall and stopped in front of her. "Can we go somewhere to talk?"

It felt like she had a choice: allow her fear to control her or face it.

"I feel like we've done this before."

"We have." He reached up and slipped a finger between the fastened buttons of her shirt, gently tugging her toward him. She stepped closer. "Only this time, I'm hoping we won't just be talking." He licked his bottom lip.

Imogene felt her cheeks heat, and her belly crash landed inside her, sparking an explosion. "Thank you for the tiny planets."

"I would do anything for you, Imogene." He ducked his head to meet her gaze. "You said you were sorry, earlier."

She nodded.

"How come?"

"Because I pushed you away." She wanted Timaeus

Kade in her life, fear be damned. "I don't want that."

"What?"

"Not having you in my life."

He grinned. "And you've talked to the Sirkuhl, now."

"You told him. About Dwellen."

"I told him about a lot of stuff. Remember I said I had an assignment. It's over now."

Suddenly the rest of the missing pieces slid into place: his reaching out to help, his concern about crossing lines, his being at the right place at the right time. She was the assignment. "Are you saying you want to kiss me now?"

"Stars, yes. I'm free and clear."

Her heart slammed up against her ribs as she continued to burn. "You gave me the puzzle box. The cipher."

"You figured it out." He leaned forward and pressed his lips to her cheek.

She inhaled his scent, the clean, fresh hint of outdoors mixed with something slightly spicy. As she grasped onto his shirt, rolled it into her fists, and held on. "You knew? About my parents? And Tsua?"

"There are some things I'm not at liberty to discuss." He pressed his lips closer to hers, then whispered, "But if you decide to accept your Legacy, I will tell you everything."

Because he was Legion.

Her lungs fluttered inside her, making it difficult to catch her breath. "What's your placement, Kade?"

"Timaeus. And officially, I will be working within the security sector of the capitol." He pulled back and looked at her.

"Officially. With Vempur?"

"Same department."

His cover.

And if she agreed to join Legion, she would have a cover.

She grabbed his hand and started walking through the corridor. "We definitely need to talk."

A few turns ago, Vempur had asked her what she wanted. She hadn't been able to answer him, but she knew now.

She wanted her place as a Legacy in whatever Legion would be. And she wanted Timaeus Kade.

Tsua—her friend—had hurt her, but ultimately, his betrayal had woken her too. She'd been moving through the motions at the Academy for seven years fighting to make her own legacy. She'd done that regardless of how things had ended up on that leaderboard. But she'd done it for all the wrong reasons. Now, in this moment, she had every intention of claiming the life she wanted, and it started with Timaeus.

She led him across the courtyard to the dorms. He followed, riding the lift to her floor. The silence between them was a vacuum extracting any additional information into its energy field, including her thoughts, as if it were a black hole. Except for Timaeus's tension. That, she could feel arching between them like its own force field. His hand tightened around hers.

She opened her door.

Timaeus followed her in.

The door slid shut.

They collided, two stars collapsing and combining their energy. Her hands were in his silky hair. His hands were on her hips, holding her tightly against him, squeezing.

As they kissed, he offered his fire, and it ignited her own: heat and desire and not enough space to be combining stars. Beautiful sounds between them, adding fuel to their fervor. They knocked things from the surface of her desk when he lifted her onto it, sent a chair rolling across the room.

"I'm so sorry," she said between kisses.

"Hush," he replied. "No talking, Ima. No talking." He pulled her hips across the desk, his mouth seeking hers once more, moaning into it and setting his hips between her open legs, sliding his hands down her thighs to her knees.

"This is more than friendship," she said against his mouth.

"I told you, I want to be so much more than your friend, Ima. Now focus."

She laughed, and his mouth strayed from her lips.

"I've wanted to do this for so long," he admitted.

"Me too."

"How long?"

"Are you competing with me?"

"Yes." He grinned against her skin and lifted her off the desk, carrying her toward her bed to lay her down. Settling on top of her, he braced his elbows on either side of her shoulders. "Everything's a competition." He grinned. "I won, by the way."

She groaned.

"Third place to your fourth."

"Dear god, you're never going to let me forget it."

"I hope, Ima, that I will get to remind you of that for the rest of our lives." His hands caressed her face before leaning down and pressing a chaste kiss to her lips.

"That's a long time," she whispered.

"I've known you for seven years, Ima. And I've been in love with you for over half of them." He searched her face with those dark, beautiful, intense, gorgeous eyes. "A lifetime doesn't feel like long enough."

"You love me, Kade?"

"It's Timaeus, Ima." He grinned and nodded, giving her another kiss, then he drew back so he could fully meet her gaze. "I do. Too soon?"

"It isn't." She pushed him so he rolled over, then climbed onto him, housing his hips between her knees as she started unbuttoning her shirt. His intense gaze tracked her movement, his hands squeezing her thighs. "I see you. I have always seen you, but I can't lie. I'm terrified."

Timaeus pulled her closer by her shirt and kissed her, penetrating her defenses until she was pliant and yielding.

They rolled again, until she was under him once more. He broke their kiss long enough to say, "But at least, Ima, we'll be facing it together."

Grasping the hem of his t-shirt, she helped him pull it over his head, her heart a rambunctious rhythm in her chest filled with hope, desire, and for the first time in a long time, joy.

"Focus, Timaeus. We have a lot of catching up to do."

Acknowledgements

Dear Readers,

I have you to thank for this book, for this book-filled journey. *The Trials of Imogene Sol* is because of you, your engagement, your willingness to support me. Way back in 2019, after *The Bones of Who We Are* released (before *The Stories Stars Tell*), I asked my Instagram followers to drop me two genre categories to inspire a story. Now, if you've been around since then, I salute you! The genre categories chosen were romance and sci fi. Romance wasn't much of a stretch but sci fi felt like I would have to travel to an unknown planet to write it. This contemporary writer was facing a challenge of the highest order!

I wrote the very first scene of this book (it's Chapter 4 now) introducing me to Imogene and Timaeus (though if you've been around since then, you know that wasn't his original name—I'm sensing a game of trivia might be in order). And somehow, Imogene's story was born, chapter-by-chapter in my newsletter over the next two years. You stuck around for it!

Thank you for being here. Thank you for buying the stories. Thank you for sharing them. Thank you for subscribing to the newsletter, for leaving reviews, for giving my books as gifts. Thank you for sharing it on social media, for engaging with me, for being active participants in my journey. I am so, so very grateful for each of you. We've made it through eleven books! Here's to eleven more.

Heartfelt thanks to my amazing family. Thank you, Kate, Beth, and Rena for your amazing work to help me. To my Carpe Diem writers' group, the beta readers who helped make this story better.

And always, all glory and honor to my God.

Cami

Playlist

Intro	Gryffin
Medium	Brambles
Cocoon	07 Shake
Freak (w/ Vandelux)	Emmit Fenn, Vandelux
Shadows in the Dark	HNTR, Elliot Moss
Asphyxia	4lienetic, Cash
Therefore I Am	Billie Eilish
Reset	SLUMP, Senbeī, Ed Tullett
I Am Freestyle	Joji
Horizon	Andrew Belle
Crossroads	Massane
Control— *Disco Lines Remix*	Emmit Fenn, Disco Lines
Reaction	GOLDHOUSE, Mokita
Amman	Emmit Fenn
Clairvoyance	ASHE
Silence (ft. Amistat)	Trivecta, Amistat
Floating	Klur
Let it Be	Hazy
Good in Me	Andy Grammer

*This playlist can be found on Spotify as "The Trials of Imogene Sol"

Coming Soon

Look for a new *Ring Academy* novel
coming soon.

Check out the following excerpt from the
upcoming low-fantasy novel:

The Memory Map

by CL Walters

The Memory Map
By CL Walters

On the night Cale's father is abducted, Cale is shoved into a hidden passageway with a map, directions to follow it. With a confession that nothing in Cale's life has been the truth and disconnected memories magically stashed in his mind by his father—magic that isn't even supposed to exist—his life upended. Cale goes to the one remaining place he feels safe—his best friend, Yoneo. But to protect Yoneo from the knowledge that could get him killed, Cale lies.

With an abridged version of the truth, Cale convinces Yoneo and their friends Jem and Domic to go on an unsanctioned trip with him to find his father. While his friends believe the lies Cale has told, he hides his true purpose to search for the truth in the magical memories triggered by each place on the map they visit. Cale realizes that like his father, he also has magical abilities, only he can't control them, putting him and his friends at greater risk. Their illegal journey, already fraught with peril as they traverse an oppressive land that *reforms* people who break the rules and kills those who are different, his inability to control his magic is a recipe for disaster, putting everyone he loves in danger.

When his lies come to light, will Cale find the bravery to face the truth, or cower in the darkness of his deceit?

PUBLISHING SOON!

ONE

Cale

The Stone Heap's crowd was boisterous and exactly what Cale needed. The smell of the hops mixed with the savory scent of stew, the laughter, and the loud conversation made it feel like the perfect place to disappear for a little while. He pulled the heavy wooden door closed behind him and looked around the establishment for his friends.

Inside of The Heap was dark and had a squat ceiling with rough-hewn wooden beams that ran the length of the room. It made him feel like he needed to crouch even if he didn't. When he considered the room full of revelers already drunk on brin and friendship, the crackle of their energy, and the lowlight making it difficult to see anyone's features with clarity, Cale might have felt claustrophobic. Instead, the need to lose himself in some brin was more powerful. A way for him to blend into the chaos of fun from the shroud of impending death that encompassed his family.

The older building was made with enormous smooth stones. Legend behind the Heap—and the whole village of Brockton, really— was passed down from old patrons to new ones. As Sir Artis Montmen—the moons provide a lighted passage to his star soul—told Cale and his best friend, Yoneo the first time they entered the tavern, "–was magic it was". He regaled them with a story about the star lovers Wyl and Tera, who, according to the old drunk, were "the parents of magic creatures, giants called the Woodyn, with the strength of twenty Junapore farmers." He claimed the Woodyn carried great heaps of stones—hence The Stone Heap—after the great River Lynd flooded the Brockton Basin way before any of them were born, when magic still existed.

Of course, Cale was skeptical. Magic? But the stones were massive. That he couldn't argue. There wasn't a way to move those stones by hand which added to the mystery of their ancient appearance. And as Sir Montmen insisted, "It was magic that carried them." He'd leaned forward and added in an exaggerated whisper. "I come from a time before it was treasonous to speak such things. Don't want an uptight Mun to overhear me," he'd said with a wink. "I'll get thrown in the Reformatory."

"Cale!"

His gaze skipped over the crowd until it landed on his best friend, Yoneo, who waved from a table in the corner where he sat with their other best mates, Jem and Domis. Yoneo smiled and flicked his hair out of his eyes with a subtle toss of his head and settled back into his seat.

Cale could read Yoneo like a book; they'd known one another so long. Right now, his friend was happy and the tell-tale red tint to his cheeks suggested he'd already had his fair share of brin.

Cale weaved his way through multitudes of patrons, many strangers, which made Cale wonder why his father agreed to let him come out to the pub as protective as he was. Though Brockton was a village on the edge of the Billerdem

Precept—Junapore's capitol since Wydyn, the larger of the two Junapore cities, was the capitol of all Anola. Billerdem was a hub for the growing industry in the territory, so it meant there were a lot of different kinds of folk in the village moving to and fro between farms, outer villages, and to the city to find work. It was one of his father's largest complaints at the loss of the tenants to the factories cropping up in need of workers. "What will happen when we have a food shortage because there aren't any farmers left to grow it?" was a common refrain.

Cale's favorite visitors were the entertainers, though many of them dealt in subterfuge considering if they were caught performing or sharing their art, they could get arrested and sent to the Reformatory by Mun agents. The Mun had long ago banned unsanctioned art. In order to share it, one had to carry permits, but due to the small nature of Brockton and the lack of interest in it by Mun officials, The Heap almost always allowed artisans a space to share with or without paperwork. As long as the moon priest wasn't present.

Cale wondered if other places like The Heap existed in Anola, but considering he couldn't go on the Grand Tour, he'd never know. He wouldn't be able to follow the trail every other young man his age in Anola, fresh from school, would get to make. Cale wondered if there were other young men like him, unable to go due to factors outside of his control. The thought made him bitter.

"By the light!" His friends said in greeting when he reached the table.

"By the light," Cale repeated and slid into the wooden booth next to Yoneo. He was thankful there was an extra cup already waiting for him.

"We weren't sure you'd come." Domis pushed the extra pint of brin toward him. The amber liquid sloshed over Domis's dark hand as he did. He grinned, but it was muted by his embarrassment and reflected in his shy, gentle smile. While Domis was a rather imposing figure at well over eighteen ruffins tall and weighed at least one hundred and eighty-five heftons, his unobtrusive nature had the power to render him invisible. "Sorry, mate." Domis offered him a crooked smile.

"No worries, Dom," Cale told his friend, picking up the tankard. "Thanks."

"Something wrong?" Jem asked.

"Besides the fact my step-mum is dying?" Cale picked up the pint and downed the whole thing. When he slammed the cup onto the wooden table with a thump, he felt all his friends watching him. Then each of them looked away, clearing their throats with varying degrees of discomfort. "Sorry," he offered. "I may not be all that fun tonight, boys."

"When are you ever?" Jem joked, his dimples cutting deeply into his pale cheeks.

"There's no pressure to change your usual pessimistic self." Yoneo raised his glass to a barmaid walking past and tapped it. She nodded. He smiled at Cale, who gave him an elbow. Then he grew serious. "She's been your mother these last seven years. I think you've got a right." His straight black hair flopped over his dark eyes, so he tossed his head. It fell right back over his eye, the strands like slick silk. "I think you have a pass for feeling something about it, you know?"

Cale swallowed.

The barmaid set down another cup. "I thought you might

use a pitcher?"

"What would we do without you?" Jem asked with a dimpled smile and twinkling gray eyes. He was a practiced and epic flirt. Most often successful with whomever he wanted to sway. When there was something that Jem wanted, there didn't seem to be a person he couldn't charm to get it.

Cale caught Domis's eyes and rolled his own.

Domis grinned, shook his head, but stayed silent. In the many years that Cale had known Domis, he'd never known him to be charming. Wicked smart, yes. Insanely focused, for sure. Loyal and trustworthy. On the whole. Charming and sociable, not so much.

The barmaid smiled back at Jem because she wasn't immune to their handsome friend's charms. "This one's on the house." She winked at Jem.

Domis turned to Jem after she walked away. "I'll never understand that." His fingers tapped against the tabletop to a rhythm only he understood. His eyes danced around never landing on anyone in particular. Dom wasn't too keen on crowds, but they'd been to The Heap enough that he'd found a way to keep himself comfortable, making it an exception.

Cale thought Jem and Domis were like two sides of a coin, each balancing out the other to be whole. Though Jem was smart in his own way, he didn't have the intellect of Domis just like Domis didn't have the charisma.

"It's a gift." Jem took a sip of his drink.

Domis chuckled while Jem smiled into his pint.

"I think you could probably charm a Simper Simper, if they existed." Yoneo smiled at the thought.

"Probably. I'd give it a good go, anyway," Jem said. "Since it would be between life and death."

"Maybe you've got magic? Philia seems to think it still exists." Cale threw the observation into the mix.

They all laughed and toasted with their pints of brin.

"Don't let an official hear you say that," Yoneo said with a wide smile, the irony hitting the right note as he was on his way to becoming a Mun official. They all laughed with him, and he picked up the pitcher and refilled everyone's tankards. He raised his pint after he'd finished and turned toward Cale. "To your mum."

Cale met his friends' gazes as their cups clinked together again. They each drank the pints all the way down—again—and were on their way toward complete inebriation. Cale could tell his cheeks were warming with the ease of the brin, and Yoneo's cheeks had turned even redder—like ripe fruit. Jem looked the same as always, handsome and charming as a devil. Domis was frowning into his tankard.

"What is it, Dom," Cale asked his friend.

"I was thinking–"

"No! No, Dom! No thinking!" Jem shouted with a laugh in his voice and punched Domis's giant shoulder.

Dom shoved him away.

Jem laughed louder as he flopped against the wall of their booth.

"You're not going to get to go on The Tour are you?" Domis asked. His dark brown eyes connected with Cale, shaded with disappointment, and his thick eyebrows slanted over his eyes with the weight.

"Don't say that." Jem set down his tankard. There wasn't much that made Jem frown, but disappointment could. His charming nature, so much like lightning in a bottle, could flip into anger like blustery thunder during a storm. "Look, boys,

I have it on good authority that the Tour is a means and a method to chaos. It is imperative we all go. One last go before everything–" he stopped before he said it. They knew change was coming, that life would never be like it once had been at school. Jem cleared his throat. "And that means you too, Cale. It's going to be legendary."

"Boys," Cale started.

Each of their voices along with their body language all jumped into the conversation adding to the chaos in the room.

"No."

"Don't even *boys*, us."

"Cale!"

"She's dying. How am I supposed to leave my father?" Unable to look at them, he kept his eyes on the tankard.

Of course he wanted to go on the Tour. It was an expectation. A rite of passage. The Mun Council had created the perfect route for male citizens to take in the beauty and diversity of Anola. A memorable trip for each young man to receive the fullest experience to understand the traditions, the culture, and the interconnectedness of their land. It was the opportunity to cull their independence, to open their minds to new places and people, and mostly to have some fun before the real world of their job training began.

Truthfully, the tales brought back by their older friends had fueled their excitement and motivated them to make it through their sixth-cycle, final, board examinations; it had become the only thing they had been talking about over the last year at Academy. That and their exploitations with the objects of their fantasies of course, but The Grand Tour had been more important than even coupling at school with people they already knew. Because what could be had on the tour? Coupling. With new people. So, they'd made plans anyway even knowing in the back of their minds that Cale probably wouldn't be able to go. They'd all dreamed and planned together anyway. That was how it was supposed to be.

Now, it was just one more thing of many being taken from him.

"You have to go, Cale. I mean, your mum could make it another year. Right?" Jem's dimples disappeared, and his usually arched dark brows straightened out over his eyes.

Domis shook his head, and he grabbed the coils of his hair; something he always did when he wanted to concentrate on the topic at hand.

"It's bad."

"So you can't go?" Yoneo frowned at his drink, then looked at Cale. "For sure?"

Cale hated to disappoint them, but he knew they would be fine. They would still go on the Tour. It would be him left behind. Again. Like always. "Aye. No traveling the continent for me. My family needs me."

"Great skies," Jem smacked the tabletop. "It's supposed to be the four of us."

Silence settled between them even though the pub was alive with noise.

Though it was painful to say, Cale said, "Well, we always knew, right? I've always been the odd man out."

The truth was his father never let Cale do much of anything. The one who couldn't go on a school trip to a distant precept of Junapore, or the one who couldn't participate in the study of watershed in Billerdem which required an overnight stay at a camp in the valley. Always a source of jokes for Cale to keep from feeling like he didn't belong, but housed inside the humor was the truth, and it was filled with bitterness that Cale could feel like the heaviness of an overripe apple ready to burst on the tree.

He was eighteen now, but how could he argue with his father, who faced a dying wife? The same man who'd raised him, sacrificed his life for him? Cale couldn't even if he wanted to because whatever selfish thing he wanted didn't measure up to the ways his father had cared for him. It was his turn to be the caretaker. To help with his little sister, Philia. To be the rock.

He offered a laugh to help his friends feel better, but it didn't sound right and drew their eyes to him instead. He swallowed. "I'm disappointed, but I don't want it to be me who messes up the plans. Okay?"

His friends didn't respond. Instead, each of them returned to staring at their drinks, mouths sunken into frowns with the gravity of reality.

Yoneo forced a smile. "Yes. For you, we'll make the grandest plans." He lifted his tankard. "I propose that at every stop we complete a task in honor of our missing Cale." His dark eyes—nearly black—slid to Cale.

Cale could see the sadness in them, the weight of sorrow that was heavier than just him not being able to go. It was burgeoning with all the ways Yoneo couldn't take away the hurt Cale would suffer from the loss of the Tour with his friends, but more the loss of Kurin. Yoneo always knew him.

Cale offered him a slight nod he knew only Yoneo would notice, then smiled. "I like it. And when you return, you will regale me with all the Cale adventures."

He listened with a smile as his friends began talking

about ways they could embody Cale in their adventures. In the Lyndloce precept of Wyden, they decided that Jem would need to find a girl to charm into tattooing Cale's name on her behind. Then when they sailed the Large Grale River, they would drink themselves into a stupor and tattoo "by the light" on their butts. This of course was Jem's addition to which Domis said "absolutely not."

"That sounds like a lot of bums and tattoos." Cale laughed.

"What else is life about but tattoos and arses?" Jem exclaimed.

They laughed and continued to regale one another with outlandish antics trying to outdo one another.

Though it hurt to know he would be missing out, he was glad they allowed him the camaraderie of feeling as though he could still be a peripheral part of their journey. He vowed to be happy for them even if he was stuck in Brockton waiting for Kurin to cross over into the light of the stars. It gave him a pang of shame to know that a part of him wanted to run away from that when his father had only ever been there for him.

So, he took another deep drink of brin and resolved to be present, right now.

That, at least, he could do.

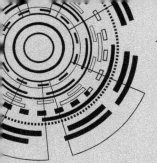

About the Author

CL Walters writes in Hawai'i where she lives with her husband, two children, and acts as a pet butler to a plethora of pampered fur-babies. She's the author of the YA Contemporary series, *The Cantos Chronicles (Swimming Sideways, The Ugly Truth* and *The Bones of Who We Are)*, the NA Contemporary romances, *The Messy Truth About Love, The Stories Stars Tell, In the Echo of this Ghost Town,* and *When the Echo Answers,* and the adult romance, *The Letters She Left Behind. The Ring Academy: The Trials of Imogene Sol* is her first jump into space and science-fiction-lite. For up-to-date news, sign up for her monthly newsletter on her website at www.clwalters.net and follow her writer's journey on Instagram @cl.walters as well as SubStack @Cami, the Author.

Printed in the USA
CPSIA information can be obtained
at www.ICGtesting.com
LVHW040357180923
758453LV00003B/317